The
Eden Book Society
100 Years of Unseen Horror

Holt House

L. G. Vey

First published in 1972
by The Eden Book Society

The Eden Book Society

First published in Great Britain in 2018 by The Eden
Book Society, an imprint of Cinder House Publishing Limited.

ISBN 978-1-911585-42-8

Printed and bound in Great Britain by Clays Ltd,
St Ives plc.

www.edenbooksociety.com

www.deadinkbooks.com

About the Society

Established in 1919, The Eden Book Society was a private publisher of horror for nearly 100 years. Presided over by the Eden family, the press passed through the generations publishing short horror novellas to a private list of subscribers. Eden books were always published under pseudonyms and, until now, have never been available to the public.

Dead Ink Books is pleased to announce that it has secured the rights to the entire Eden Book Society backlist and archives. For the first time, these books, nearly a century of unseen British horror, will be available to the public. The original authors are lost to time, but their work remains and we will be faithfully reproducing the publications by reprinting them one year at a time.

We hope that you will join us as we explore the evolving fears of British society as it moved through the 20th century and eventually entered the 21st. We begin our reproduction with 1972, a year of exciting and original horror for the Society.

L. G. Vey

L.G. Vey was born in Southampton in 1921. He served in the Royal Engineers during World War II, and then joined the British Broadcasting Corporation, starting his career in television as a technician. By the end of the 1950s he was an award-winning scriptwriter with a number of well-known horror and science fiction dramas to his name, many of which can no longer be found.

He lived, unmarried, in Hampshire for many years, where he enjoyed walking his Bassett Hounds, fishing, and painting landscapes. He died in 1978. Holt House was his only piece of fiction.

Chapter One

The branches of the wild cherry trees, thick with frothy blossom, swayed in the fierce breath of the wind. But when Ray put his eye back to the hole in the fence he couldn't see a blade of grass stir. The Latches' garden was sheltered from the breeze: orderly, maintained, perfect.

The lawn was cut short. He had watched Mr Latch mow it a dozen times or more, carefully pushing along a cylindrical lawnmower that looked pre-war. It fascinated Ray how he never saw the blades of grass grow; time was an invisible process in this place. The Latches had aged, were aging, but he couldn't see it, and the house, with its large rectangular windows and gabled back porch, the mossy slope of its high roof and the two thin chimneys, looked exactly the same to him as it had when he was eleven years old.

He had been so very scared, then.

The dusky pink curtains in one of the upper rooms – the Latches' bedroom, Ray assumed – were pulled back, and Ray glimpsed Mrs Latch's white, curly hair and the baby blue sleeves of the cardigan she favoured: it was only for a moment, and then she stepped back out of view.

'I'm here,' he said.

He did not move.

Close by, a wood pigeon made its calm, even call. The stalks of the bluebells, not yet erupted into flower, rustled behind him, giving away that some sort of animal was nearby. He thought a fox, or an otter, perhaps. Then he remembered that there were no more otters here, in Holtwood. There hadn't been wild otters in these parts since he was a child. Before that, even.

He did not take his eye from the hole in the fence.

The back door of the house squeaked as it was opened, and the beat of wings sounded overhead as the wood pigeon fluttered away in instant response. Mr Latch emerged, already dressed. The only difference between the past and the present was his smooth bald head – Ray's memory of him included thinning silver hair, brushed carefully from a side parting. Apart from that he was a familiar sight, from the braces stretched over his stomach to his brown leather slippers.

Mr Latch shuffled down the path that led from the back porch to the outhouse – a small stone building with peeling green paint upon the door – and as he went inside Ray thought of the new estate that was eating up chunks of the Holtwood, speeding towards change at a rate that only humans and their machines could manage. Those houses had every manner of modern convenience. He had walked around the new roads with their turning circles and cul-de-sacs, seen the kids in the play park, their feet crunching upon loose chippings around the base of the shiny swing set and the roundabout. All modern conveniences were expected; an outside lavatory, nowadays? It would never be tolerated.

He heard the flush, and Mr Latch emerged, closing the door of the outhouse behind him. He returned down the crazy-paved path to the house. Breakfast, no doubt, awaited him.

The day had started.

The Latches would eat eggs and toast, and drink tea from a brown earthenware teapot that she would warm first, then cover with a knitted cosy. The washing up would follow, and other household tasks. She would hang out the wet clothes at some point; it was going to be a fine day. She always hung the shirts out first, shaking them, and then pinning them upside down from the line that ran above the kitchen window to a pole half-way down the path.

Mr Latch would take care of that lawn, and spend time in his shed. That was what he did. Every day.

Ray crawled back from the fence, on his hands and knees. Once he was within the wood, under the cover of the trees, he stood up, and made his way back to his tent.

*

I don't know why I came back here. Where it went wrong.
To find the Latches still living here – it's a gift. Maybe

this was meant to be all along. Just like finding that hole in their fence. It's perfect for watching him. Seeing how he is.

He's the same.

When you watch someone, you know them. You know them better than they know themselves. You can get answers to all sorts of questions, without ever having to ask them directly.

But you can't get an answer to everything.

I should have paid as much attention to Trish, and watched her every day. I would have seen it come over her – the minute she decided to leave me. I would have cottoned on to what she was trying to tell me when we walked along Southsea and she asked me to buy her that shell at one of the gift shops, the big pink conch with the shiny mother of pearl inside. You'd never find one like that actually on Southsea beach. They must have shipped it in for the tourists. I bought it though, and gave it to her, and she gave it back to me, right then, on the spot. She said – it's for you to keep. To remind you of today.

I thought it was soppy, in that way that women like to be. I didn't get it at all. What she was telling me. Why I'd need a reminder of a good day, after she'd gone. She already knew she was going to go. She had it planned all along.

Everything happens for a reason.

*

Holt House

Ray put his notebook and pen back in his rucksack with the shell from Southsea. He remembered how, after buying the shell for her, she had wanted to sunbathe although clouds had been constantly passing over the sun, and the wind had been strong. It was a pebbled beach, too – not comfortable for sitting. Still, he tried to give her whatever she wanted. He had watched the ferries make pace across the waves, in and out of the harbour. Then he had glanced at her, lying on the pebbles, arms and legs flung out wide, her skirt pulled up to her thighs.

Put your legs away, he had said, not wanting other men to see her that way. Had that been wrong? Her expression had darkened, but deep down he thought she enjoyed it: his jealousy over her, his need to keep her for himself.

The next day he had set sail on Ark Royal for a NATO exercise. He'd been gone for four months. It hadn't even been a long stint, compared to the usual, but it was long enough.

He took the Polaroid of her from his shirt pocket, kissed it, and replaced it. He reached for his wash bag before backing out of the tent, closing up the canvas loops, and making his way down to the river.

*

The River Meon formed a natural barrier between the new estate and Holt House, winding through a number of Hampshire villages until it found its way to the Solent.

But here, high in the Holtwood, it was knee deep and silty, cold and with a perceptible current after the spring storm last week.

Ray stripped off and waded in.

He washed this way every morning, but he still smelled bad all the time. It wasn't his clothes. He had washed them, too, and hung them from the trees. It was a deep down smell inside him. It was no wonder that he never saw any animals; they must be able to sniff him out miles away. Foxes and badgers surely still thrived here – he had seen the holes, tracks and trails – even if the otters were all gone. Maybe they watched him. Maybe they wished him gone.

When Dad had brought him to this very spot in the river, and they had waited patiently to see otters, they had no idea that they could have hidden in the leaves forever and never got lucky. They had spent hours out here, when Mum was at her worst during the pregnancy, and Dad would say, *It'll be today, I'm sure.* A flash of brown, a swipe of a long tail, as quick and smooth as an eel: sometimes Ray even convinced himself that he had seen one. *There. There. He's still there, look.* Dad would shake his head.

It wouldn't hang around for you to point him out. Otters are fast. So fast. All the other animals are afraid of them, did you know that? They're carnivores, with teeth that can go through bone. If you see one, stay down, and stay quiet.

Holt House

Going near one never was an option, but the hunt kept them talking when everything else was too difficult to discuss. One time, though, they saw a kingfisher. A dot of electric blue, hovering, and then zipping away on tiny pulses of energy. That had been close to the Latches' house, by the fence. They had walked past there many times, on the way to the river.

Ray finished washing. He shook out water from his hair, and felt the growth of it. His beard was thickening too, day by day.

The wind dropped, leaving a hole in the usual sounds of the wood: no birdsong, no rustling. At such moments he felt certain he was being observed. It wasn't just the thought of the animals he never saw. It was as if the trees, the water, the wood itself had eyes upon him.

He waded back to the bank, aware of the way he disturbed the river, making patterns in a place that should be free of human interference.

*

The space behind the Latches' fence was beginning to look like the den of some animal. The springy grass that grew around the posts had been flattened by his body weight. A man who knew what to look for could see signs of life here, could even follow them back to his tent.

They won't look for you here, he reminded himself. *You're safe.*

He sat in his spot, and put his eye to the hole in the fence.

Mr Latch was sitting on the wooden bench under the kitchen window, smoking his pipe.

Time played its usual trick in the presence of Holt House: each puff the old man took was languorous; each raise of the stem to the droop of his lower lip was poised; every curl of smoke took an age to rise to the sky, and dissipate.

Latch was dressed in his usual outfit. His stomach pushed out against the material of his shirt and trousers, and his braces curved around it. The same old brown leather slippers remained in place, and there were grey woollen socks underneath, with a stripe of skin visible above each ankle where the trousers rode up.

Where was Mrs Latch? Ray never saw her at this time of day, but the bedroom curtains were closed again so he assumed she took a nap after lunch. But even if she had been sitting next to her husband, they would not have spoken. They hardly ever spoke.

It wasn't how he remembered them from that night when they had taken him into their house. They had worn concerned smiles, considerate expressions, as they welcomed him and assured his dad that they would take care of Ray for as long as was needed. She had carried on talking to his dad in the hall while Mr Latch had said, 'Young man, I'm sure we can find something to interest you,' leading him away to the kitchen, for biscuits. When she joined them, they had held a little conversation about what to do, what blankets to put on the spare bed, that kind of thing, but he had sensed even back then that the words had been pitched for his ears, in light and soothing tones.

For a small boy like him, in an emergency, the public face of the Latches had been presented. Alone, thinking there was nobody to see them, their mouths sat a little slacker.

The pipe finished, Mr Latch knocked it out on the arm of the bench, pocketed it, and then made his way down the path towards Ray's spot behind the fence. The shed, of course: he was going to the shed, as he did every afternoon. It was a small, flat-topped wooden shack that Ray couldn't see from his hiding place, but he had been taken into it as a child, on that one visit, and he remembered it clearly.

One window, with a workbench beneath it, had given a view back towards the house. An old tea chest had squatted in the corner, along with a pile of wood offcuts. At the back of the shed had been a set of hooks that held tools, metal things, and then two rows of shelves bearing cobwebbed jam jars filled with nuts, bolts, screws, washers, buttons, clips.

Banging brought Ray back to the here and now. Mr Latch was creating in his shed. Ray pictured him selecting the claw hammer from the rack of tools on hooks. Perhaps he was pounding nails into wood. He had shown Ray a nailed construction that day – *a fort*, he had said, but it had looked like no recognisable object.

And then he had taken him indoors, and shown him the wardrobe. The thing inside.

That sick, cornered feeling reappeared as, in a flash of memory, Latch whispered to him once more. What were the words? He couldn't remember. He couldn't remember.

He crawled away, his hands balled into fists, and was sick beside the trunk of a cherry tree. The wood whispered around him.

*

It had only been a small shop, once. But since his childhood it had been expanded back and back, shelves stacked high, to double as a post office, newsagent, and sweet shop, amongst other things. Ray guessed the latter incarnation was popular with the kids off the local estate; a pile of Choppers had been dumped just outside the door when he arrived, and the boys inside were waiting for a quarter of aniseed balls to be measured out from one of the tubs behind the counter.

'Kids,' said the man serving, once they had left. He was thick-set, with sleeves rolled up to reveal a tattoo of a rose inside his left arm, just below the elbow. Ex-military,

Ray suspected. He wondered if the man thought the same of him. 'They're all right at that age, but give 'em a year and they'll be in here trying to pinch everything they can reach. That's why I put the expensive stuff higher up.' He gestured to the top shelves, which held a range of cans and packets that looked no different than the ones on the lower shelves to Ray. 'Seen you round here a bit. You moved in somewhere?'

'No no, just visiting a relative.'

'Oh yeah? Who's that, then?'

'How much are the cans of beans?'

'Price should be on the bottom.'

'Oh yeah, thanks.' Ray made a show of checking the sticky label, and put what he wanted into his wire basket. Beans, soup, canned fruit. A few Fry's chocolate bars, for energy.

'It's the parents,' said the man, as he tallied up the cost of the goods on pen and paper beside the till. 'Too busy watching television to pay attention, not even caring whether they get on the bus to go to school every day. I've got a lad that age. You have to keep an eye on them. Give them stuff to do.'

'Isn't it Saturday?' said Ray, suddenly fearful that he had lost count of the days out in the wood.

'Yeah, no, it's Saturday. Getting on to lunchtime. We're just about to close up.' The man threw him a look as he handed him a plastic bag containing his purchases, and

Ray knew he'd made a mistake. Now he was memorable. He'd have to find another shop – walk further, to the next village along, or even make the journey into Bishops Waltham to visit the Co-op.

When he left the shop the Choppers were gone, and the street was quiet. The garage next to the shop was shut up tight. He idled past and, through the large window to the customer area, saw a slew of curling newspapers on a low coffee table, with a few chairs arranged around it. On the orange partition wall was a pinned picture from a newspaper, showing a woman sitting in a field, naked, her body hidden by the red dabs of wild poppies, apart from a tantalising view of the side of one breast. He stopped and stared at her untouchable smile.

When he was young there hadn't been a customer area. The only picture in the garage had been of the Queen. It had hung in a heavy frame on the wall behind the pits and the tools and the tyres. He remembered it clearly, from when his father took in the Allegro for a service. *It has to be tip-top*, said his dad. *For when the baby finally comes.*

Ray, in the grip of memory, walked away. He turned left, then right, to find his feet upon a familiar lane.

It was a mile or so to stroll in bright sunlight and a blustery wind. What had been meadows fifteen years ago were now lined, ploughed fields, with the green fuzz of new spring growth just beginning to erupt. A barbed wire fence had been strung along the roadside to deter those who would walk over the land and ruin its symmetry. When Ray reached the house he kept back, close to the barbed wire, and surveyed it.

Canary yellow paint coated the door and window sills, although the walls themselves remained white. But it was a bigger, bolder house in many ways – a new car port sat on one side, and on the other was a two-storey extension in a different brick entirely, jutting out, capped with its own red roof.

How was it that Holt House, and the Latches, had escaped time, but his own family home had not?

An upstairs window opened. It had once been his parents' bedroom, but now an unknown woman leaned out, and said, 'Can I help? Are you lost?'

How long had he been standing there? He turned and walked away, fast, further along the pitted, dry road until he could be certain he was out of her line of sight.

The barbed wire stretched on, unbroken, for minute after minute. He refused the urge to look behind him. He remembered hearing his mother, wailing, wailing in that upstairs bedroom; it had sounded like torture was being committed upon her swollen stomach. And then there had been the sound of the siren: the arrival of the ambulance. *Aren't you going in the car?* he asked his dad, and heard: *It's too late for that.* Plans had been made and they were left unused. There had been a pram, his old pram, brought down from the attic and cleaned up by himself and his dad, together. His dad wheeled it to the end of the garden and let it sit there, in all weathers, afterwards. The spokes had bloomed red rust.

I've got to go be with your mum, said Dad, as the ambulance men headed up the stairs. *The Latches won't mind having you tonight, I bet. It's just for tonight.*

Ray stopped walking.

The beginning of crop growth covered everything, where once there had been so many flowers: cornflowers, campions, catmint. Hadn't he found a dormouse, once, nestled in stalks? Curled up tight. Secure. Safe.

He grasped the barbed wire, between the spikes, and hoisted himself over. The bottom of his flared jeans caught, throwing him off-balance; he pitched forward, against the new growth and the dirt. The material gave, ripped away, and when he sat up he could see a strip of the faded blue denim left on the wire, snagged, bearing witness to his presence. He scrabbled at his foot, expecting to see blood, but there was nothing.

Nobody's looking for you here, he reminded himself.

He got up and strode back in the direction of the woods, planting his feet, crushing the tender crops with deliberation.

*

Stupid. I've been stupid, to leave so many traces of myself behind. People will remember me. If they get asked, they'll say:

oh yes, there was this bloke. He stood out like a sore thumb. He wasn't one of us. He wasn't normal.

I need to get on with it. What I came here to do. I need to know how he lives with what he did to me without a trace of it showing on him. How can he look the same? Exactly the same?

He marked me.

I never thought about this stuff once I'd joined up. I was too busy. And then out at sea, seeing the world, working so hard every day. I pushed the thought of that bloody wardrobe so far away from me, it didn't seem real. The smell of it, the way it felt. What the hell was it?

She was my security against having to think of it. And now she's taken all that from me, and I see it and feel it all over again. But I don't know what it is I'm seeing and feeling and I'm going mad with it. This is what it is to go mad.

I bet she's shacked up with someone else. I bet she never gives me a second thought. She's fine, she's happy, and I'm here. The dreams aren't real. It's just whatever was in that wardrobe, spilling over into my memories. That's all it is.

*

Sunset.

Ray put his eye to the hole in the fence. It was the sweet spot in the evening when Mrs Latch regularly switched on the light in the kitchen, but hadn't yet got around to

L. G. Vey

drawing the curtains. He could see her, standing at the window, her head bowed. She was washing up the dishes from dinner, of course; he knew the position of the sink, and could picture it clearly. It was an old-fashioned basin with a wall-mounted heater on the wall by the window, with a long pipe for hot water. While she cleaned the plates, knives and forks, Mr Latch would–

Yes, here he was. Right on time, in the last rays of the day. The porch door opened and he stood there, stretching his arms out wide, tilting back his chin.

'Time for a smoke,' said Ray.

Mr Latch shuffled over to the bench. He took out his pipe, tobacco pouch, and matches, and began the business of lighting up.

There it was: slowed time, nothing moving, nothing moving. Ray placed his hands against the fence, fingers spread, and breathed in and out in time with the puffs of the pipe.

If only he could have an honest conversation with Latch. All he wanted was to stand up and cross to him, the fence no longer a barrier or a hiding place, and say easily and clearly: *What happened that night, when I stayed?*

'She left me,' he whispered.

The old man cocked his head, then nodded. Had he heard? Did he understand? Ray felt his heart shudder in his chest, a spasm of fear and longing; then he realised – it was an owl, the raucous screech of a barn own, nearby, that held Latch's attention.

Holt House

The smoke finished, the pipe was tapped out on the arm of the bench. Latch said, loudly, 'Barn's out, Gwen.' He walked back to the house, and closed the door behind him.

It meant something, it had to mean something: this speaking aloud for the first time in Ray's earshot. It felt as if it was meant for him rather than for Mrs Latch, to let him know something was different after all. Something was going to happen, change was coming. Time was unpicking itself from the walls of Holt House, removing its protective barrier.

*

Nearly a month here. The spring nights mean spending less and less time in the dark. I wouldn't mind a bit more dark. I might feel better wrapped up in it, burrowed and small, like that dormouse.

When I'm not seeing red everywhere I'm seeing her face. The bad stuff, the way her face hardened against me, and her mouth spat out words with her lips thinned.

It's not even her I'm angry at, really. It's the neighbours, who don't see her for a few days and call the police. They don't trust me.

Maybe, if I went back to Portsmouth now, she would be there. Back. That would be like putting two fingers up to the lot of them. She would say she was wrong to leave me, and beg me to forgive her. And I could go back to work, see Captain Turner and explain, and he would understand the pressure I was under, and say it was water under the bridge.

Like he would ever say that to any one of us lads.

I'm dreaming, dreaming with my eyes open, I know it. It's too late for all that, and it's too late to pretend that I've just been camping out here rather than waiting. Waiting for the right time to get into that house and get my answers.

I think the right time is coming. I think it's nearly here.

*

He woke early, at dawn, with a strange, earthy taste in his mouth. For a moment he lay there, listening, trying to place the sound in the distance that had jerked him from a dream of the wardrobe.

Someone was screaming.

No. The high wail of a siren was penetrating the Holtwood. He had the sense that everything – the animals, the insects, the trees – had stopped moving to listen to it.

It was getting closer.

He sat up in his sleeping bag and scrabbled for his clothes.

They were coming for him.

He laced his boots, grabbed his pack, and took off at a blind run towards the river, trying to put distance between himself and the siren. Getting closer. He couldn't outrun it. He blundered into a thicket of brambles, ripped himself free, feeling the sting of tiny spikes in his skin. Abruptly, he found himself at the bank of the river. The siren was upon him; then it ceased.

Ray tried to slow his breathing.

The wood was silent. Natural noises began to return: the water running past, the wind in the branches, the birds.

The feeling of being watched stole over him, and prickled at his awareness. He didn't move. He scanned, with his eyes, over the edge of the far bank.

There it was. A tiny movement gave it away. The vague shapes of leaves and grass coalesced into a brown curve, a black nose, paws. Two eyes.

An otter.

It was crouching low, alert through every line of its body, its gaze on him. He had never seen a creature so intent. It was poised to flee, or attack: its wildness was powerful. He felt it as an awareness between them. His hands trembled. He couldn't stop them from shaking, but didn't dare to move them, not even to clench them into fists.

The otter broke its gaze upon him, and looked away with a sudden disinterest: a judgement. It dropped into the river, smooth and clean, without a splash, and he watched as it passed him by, heading downstream, underwater, a graceful streak of muscle.

It churned up a curious wake behind it; the usually clear water looked muddy, brownish. Red. Was the otter bleeding?

'Stay,' he whispered.

It stopped moving, was still, under the water. For all the world it could have been a stone, or a rag. Not a living, breathing animal. He kept his eyes fixed upon it. Blood unspooled from its back leg, like loose thread. He knelt by the bank, and put his hands into the river.

It would turn on him, it would bite him, there would be pain. He touched the fur on its back. It was firm, slick. He tried to move his fingers down to the bleeding leg, and then the otter twisted, wrapped around his hand, and he realised it was not alive, not dead, not a creature at all. A piece of material, brown, tangled around his wrist. He lifted it, and muddy water ran down over the cuff of his shirt.

It was fur. A piece of an old fur coat, maybe.

He flung it away, back into the river, and stood up.

The siren. What if it hadn't been for him at all?

He started back towards the Latches' house.

*

He could see the brown leather slippers.

The body was lying on the path outside the toilet. A dark blue blanket covered the face and the torso, leaving only the feet exposed. Those grey socks and the slippers were still in place.

Two men in blue shirts were standing close to where Mr Latch had fallen. They were facing away from Ray,

Holt House

towards the house; he could only see their backs, and the small movements of their shoulders. As they shifted apart, he caught a glimpse of Mrs Latch, nodding her head at them as they talked. It was a soft conversation. He could hear none of it.

An open bag sat on the path, and equipment lay inside, but Ray couldn't see it clearly. Medical, he guessed. Two dark blue hats, like the kind ambulance men wore, were beside it. That made sense.

Then one of the men stepped backwards, and gave Ray a clear view of her. She may have been nodding still, but her eyes were on the fence – did she see him? No. But something about the fence, very close to the hole, had her attention. How tame and cowed she looked. He had never had such an opportunity to look full at her face before. She was usually moving around, cleaning, preparing things for her husband.

She looked just as he remembered her from his childhood, except around the eyes. Her eyes looked very tired to him.

She stopped nodding, and the men's shoulders stopped moving up and down. They were no longer talking to her. They retrieved their hats, and put them on. Then they followed Mrs Latch back into the house.

The body was left behind.

'What did you do to me?' he said, as loud as he dared, speaking only to himself now there was no way to get the

21

answer he needed. 'What did you do?' He repeated it, over and over, until they returned with a stretcher and took the body away.

Chapter Two

Her eyes brightened at his name.

'Of course I remember you!' she said. 'Little Raymond. You were such a nice boy.'

'I just wanted to say – I'm sorry for your loss.'

She had a small handkerchief, lacy, poking out from the sleeve of her favourite cardigan. Ray drank up the details of her that he hadn't been able to appreciate from the fence line: her voice, her smile, and the gold bands of the wedding and engagement rings that had worn her finger thin. She took out the hanky and dabbed it under her nose.

'Thank you,' she said, 'that's very kind. Look at you! All grown up.'

'Yeah, I'm in the Navy now.'

'Are you really?'

'Is there anything you need? Anything I can do to help?'

She shrugged. 'I don't really know where to start with any of it, to be honest, dear. I had some papers through from the hospital.'

'Do you want me to take a look? I remember the paperwork – I helped my dad with it a bit after my mum…'

'Oh yes, of course,' Mrs Latch said, her face falling naturally into sympathy, and with that she opened the front door and stepped back to admit him. It was as simple as that. Even with his dirty clothes and his beard, his backpack slung over one shoulder and that smell of rot still spilling out of him, she let him in.

Standing in the hallway made a boy of him once more. Nothing had changed. The carpet was a rich green, and the yellow Anaglypta wallpaper held a pattern of diamonds. Next to the dark oak banisters of the staircase was a grandfather clock, a fine old example with an ornate face, that gave a rich ticking to the room.

The plates, Ray remembered best. They were mounted along the wall opposite the staircase, in a row, and they depicted otters in a stylised fashion, one to each plate, facing to the left, showing only one eye that sat precisely in the centre. Their bodies were twisted to fit the circular space, curled against varying backgrounds of delicate leaves and flowers.

'Come through,' said Mrs Latch, as she shut the door behind him.

He had a clear memory of having to walk under the stare of those otters when he was a boy; now, he was tall enough to look down upon them as he passed them by.

The kitchen was the same, too. It was a long, thin room with a high ceiling. Close to the door was a sturdy Welsh dresser, in shadow, next to a round table and four matching chairs which had to be squeezed past in order to get to the cupboards, cooker and sink. Only that far half of the room had light; it poured in through the kitchen window. Ray walked over to the sink and looked out at the garden.

It seemed so much larger from this vantage point. The outhouse couldn't be seen at all; the view was obscured by the jutting edge of the back porch, which made it look as if that perfect lawn stretched away forever, beyond his vision. The shed was visible, though, and that was showing signs of decay. The roof had partially collapsed, and the wooden slatted walls leaned inwards, as if the structure had slumped under the weight of its age.

The fence ran neatly behind the shed, without a trace of weeds or overgrowth around it. Ray could just make out the hole, behind which he had crouched. How obvious it seemed, from here. He supposed that the Latches hadn't even seen it.

'Would you like tea?'

'Yes please, that would be lovely.' He moved out of her way, and retreated to take a seat at the table. The tablecloth was clean and white. He smoothed it with his hands as she boiled the kettle on the stove, and warmed the teapot.

'Have you contacted the funeral home yet, Mrs Latch?'

'No, I, do I do that? I couldn't remember. No, of course, I do that, don't I?'

'That's right.' He thought of his dad, making the arrangements after that night. 'I can get the telephone number for you. Or I'll call for you, if you like.'

'I wouldn't know where to start myself,' she admitted. She collected objects on a melamine tray and put them in front of him: a teacup on a saucer, a small spoon, a bowl of sugar, a jug of milk.

'It's fine,' he said, as an automatic reaction, but he had no idea how it would be, or what he even meant by it. Still, it seemed to soothe her. She delivered the earthenware teapot, wrapped in its cosy, to the table, and sat down beside him.

'It was his heart, they said. The two young men who came to help.'

'Really?' Ray schooled himself, his reactions. He had to be sure not to give away that he had been there, seen it himself.

'It was only yesterday. It feels like it happened a long time ago, isn't that peculiar? Last night felt like such a very long night.'

It had been for Ray, too. Lying there in the tent, wondering what he was going to do next, twisting in his sleeping bag and in his mind, thinking such terrible thoughts, vivid, against the dark.

Then it had struck him, in the dawn light: he could still get his answers. Mr Latch may have died, but he could get inside and find the wardrobe. Whatever it was that had repulsed him, changed him, would be there; he would have put money on it. They looked like a couple that threw nothing away.

'That's normal,' he said. 'For time to seem a bit out of kilter, after a death.'

'Is it?' She looked surprised at that. 'You would know, of course, Raymond. Your mother was such a lovely woman. And to lose a little baby sister as well, at the same time.' The handkerchief came out again, from her sleeve, and was dabbed under her nose. 'How is your father doing?'

'He died last year,' said Ray. He didn't mention how they had already practically lost touch years ago, doing little more than exchanging birthday and Christmas cards. His father hadn't approved of his choice to join the Navy, and had liked Trish even less. *You two are trouble together*, he had said, once.

'Ahhhh,' she said, and reached over the table to pat his hand. 'Death is very cruel, isn't it? I think we should pass a law, and get rid of it.'

'I'd be happy with that.'

She smiled at him. Thoughts of doing whatever it took to get his answers were difficult to hold in his head when she looked at him that way, as if they were both victims left in the wake of the disaster called death. For the first time he wondered if Mr Latch had made her look into the wardrobe as well. Would she tell him, if she had suffered at her husband's hands? Could he win her trust?

'Ernie needed to go for a tinkle, I suppose,' she said, suddenly, leaning in close to him. 'The sound of him going downstairs didn't wake me. It takes a lot to wake me up once I'm asleep. So he could have been calling for me, shouting, and I wouldn't have heard.'

''There's no reason to blame yourself.'

She shook her head at him, quite crossly, but continued in her mild voice, 'He wasn't well, you see. I knew it, I should have paid attention. I woke up, like a shock, with a gasp. I can't explain it, dear. I knew something was wrong. I knew it. I went downstairs and out to the loo, and he was on the path, not moving. I could tell he had gone. It wasn't him any more. So I came back inside and telephoned the ambulance.' She took a deep breath. 'I never wanted to have a telephone, but Ernie said it would come in useful one day, and he was right, wasn't he? *Remember your 999*, he said. *Modern ambulances can work wonders.* But it wasn't enough, was it? It doesn't change the fact that when your time is up, your time is up.'

'It's been very upsetting for you,' said Ray. 'I don't think you should be alone.'

'There's nobody else, though. But don't worry about me, dear, I'll be fine. I'll soldier on.'

'Listen. My house is being decorated, and I was going to stay in a hotel, but maybe, if you're all right with it, I could keep you company for a few days instead. Just to get arrangements sorted.'

'Oh, yes please, Raymond, yes please,' she said, then stood abruptly and shuffled to the sink. She clutched its straight sides as her shoulders shook. He heard her gulping, struggling to suppress her emotions.

'Okay then. That's settled. No need to worry. I'll take care of it all.'

He thought of his mother. She would still be young, compared to Mrs Latch. But he couldn't help but feel that there was some connection – that helping Mrs Latch would make his mother happy. And Trish, too. All women. All the women that had left him.

Mrs Latch – Gwen – turned back to him, and gave him a smile. 'Why don't you put your bag in the spare room, dear? Get your things sorted. Maybe take a nap. You look tired. And we have lots of time for catching up. Whenever you're ready. I'll get lunch on the go.'

The spare room.

Where the wardrobe stood.

*

I don't understand women. Why they stay, why they go. I never told Trish what my dad said about us being trouble together. That's why I couldn't stand it when she said just about the same thing. Bad apart and worse together, that's how she put it. Those long stretches out at sea with my job, and then I would come back and want to know what she'd been doing, and she would never tell me. Why wouldn't she just tell me?

My mum — if she could have chosen to live, would she have wanted to? I don't remember much about her. She was ill a lot. In bed, suffering. Who would choose pain over rest?

Would she have refused to die if I'd asked her to?

She wasn't meant to have you, Dad said, over baked beans and toast. The three bar heater in the front room was on full. It must have been a harsh winter, but I don't remember what was happening outside the window. Her body wasn't strong enough for one, let alone two. She had to be stitched back together, after having me. I felt so guilty about that, even though I didn't really know what it meant.

I thought he was blaming me. Later, I worked out he was busy blaming himself and just dragging me along for the ride.

That was when I stopped telling him things. Even before the wardrobe.

If she survived after having me, survived being sewn back after being ripped to pieces, why couldn't she do it again? Why did she have to leave?

But Mrs Latch doesn't leave. She stays. She lives on, without her husband, without anything but this empty house.

I will never understand why some women leave, and some stay.

*

Ray put down the pen and thought about tearing out the page. The words he'd written were so self-centred and ridiculous. He knew he was reading too much into everything, not seeing the world as it really was.

He looked around him, at the same room where he had stayed as a boy. It looked no different through older eyes. There was a pen and ink drawing of a river winding through trees, plain and unremarkable. There was the small oak dressing table with an oval mirror fixed to it, dusty, reflecting his face back at him. And there was the rocking chair by the window, with a blue folded blanket upon the seat, faded from the sunlight.

Even though it was so familiar, he still couldn't remember exactly what had happened there. The closeness of the memory was infuriating. He willed himself to be calm.

The wardrobe was gone.

It had been tall, with thick doors and a brass keyhole without a key, and had stood opposite the bed on squat feet that curved outwards. It held his answers. He was certain of it. Ray crossed to the spot where it had stood. Yes, there were marks on the burgundy carpet. Indentations made through time. It had been there, but where had it gone?

There was a jangle of sound from the hall, demanding attention. The doorbell. He strode out to the landing and began to make his way down the stairs, body tensed, half expecting it to be the police.

Gwen was already at the door. Ray paused, two steps up from the bottom of the staircase, as she opened it.

It was the man from the local shop. His face was schooled into an expression of polite sympathy, and he held a large cardboard box. Behind him stood a young lad, dressed in a grey school uniform with a striped tie, askew. He shifted his weight from one laced-up shoe to the other.

'Hello, Trevor,' said Gwen. 'This is a surprise.'

'I thought I'd make your delivery myself this week. Just to say – we heard your news. In the village. There's a card in the top of the box.' He held it out. It looked heavy.

Ray stepped up to the door, beside Gwen, and took it.

'Thanks,' said the shopkeeper. His expression was comically surprised. 'I, er…'

'I'm just helping out for a few days,' Ray told him. 'Making sure Mrs Latch is okay.'

'Right, that's great. I'm glad, because the boy and I were worried about her, on her own. Weren't we, Jimmy?' The lad nodded, with his eyes fixed on the ground. 'He's just been to the doctor, that's why he's out of school. But he'll be right as rain, and back on deliveries next week, as usual. Just let me know if you want to change anything, change amounts, or…'

Gwen stood there, nodding, her hand on the door handle as the shopkeeper went on, speaking only to Ray. It was strange how easy it was to have a conversation as if Gwen wasn't there at all, even though it was all about her: her needs, her loss.

'Are you are a relative, then?'

'Well,' said Ray, 'I'm a friend of the family.'

'I've known Raymond for years,' said Gwen, suddenly.

'Right. That's nice. You come up from Portsmouth?'

'What makes you say that?' said Ray.

Trevor folded his arms over his chest. 'Two blokes came in the shop yesterday afternoon, just after you'd gone, and said they were looking for someone. They had a photo. I thought it looked like you. They said they'd come up from Portsmouth, and they looked military to me. You Navy?'

'I was.'

'Takes one to know one. I was Army, myself. So did they catch up with you? I said I'd thought I'd seen you. If they come back, I could point them in this direction.'

'He's trying to have a few days off from rowdy friends,' said Gwen. 'Would you mind not saying anything, Trevor, dear? At least until I feel better. It's all been a terrible shock.'

'Course,' said Trevor. 'You need some peace and quiet, after what's happened.'

'That's right.' Gwen's voice was no-nonsense. 'Do you need me to pay up the account?'

'No, no, there's no rush for that.'

'Goodbye, then.' She shut the door firmly on Trevor and his son. Ray caught a last glimpse of their bemused faces as they were left on the doorstep. 'Lunch would be cold already if it had been hot. Right, bring that through to the kitchen and wash up,' Gwen told him. Her irritation surprised him.

'Right,' said Ray. 'Yeah.' He followed her, and found a spread upon the table. Bread and butter had been cut into neat triangles, and arranged on a green plate. There was corned beef, cut fine, and a few small tomatoes, halved, that looked under-ripe, the edges scalloped into a pattern. Perhaps preparing the spread had been a good distraction from her grief; she seemed determined to keep busy.

'Is there any cheese in that box?'

He put it on the Welsh dresser, and opened up the flaps. A white envelope sat on top of a range of vegetables and fruits, and something bulky wrapped in greaseproof paper that Ray thought might be sausages. A carton of washing powder and a cake of Imperial Leather were tucked down one side. He delved in, found a block of waxy cheddar, and passed it to Gwen. She took it to the chopping board by the sink.

'Sit down and start. Hands first, of course.'

So he washed his hands, then sat and ate, swallowing down slices of corned beef and bread like a starving man.

*

After, Gwen said, 'Go sit in the garden and I'll bring you a cup of tea. It's sunny out.'

She was right. It was quite hot, on the bench, sheltered from the usual spring breeze. Ray looked down the path to the small hole in the fence. He couldn't escape the feeling that if he got up and looked through it, he would find himself there, spying on the house as usual.

Gwen brought out the tea and sat next to him. 'It's a lovely spot, here.'

'Yeah.'

'I feel very much better knowing you're here.'

'I'm glad.'

'Could I tell you something, Raymond?'

'Of course.'

She retrieved the handkerchief again, and pressed it to her lips. 'Sometimes I've thought it might be nice to be alone. I never have been alone, you see. But now I think maybe it wouldn't suit me after all. I like to have someone to look after.'

He thought about his time in the woods. 'Life can be very lonely, I've found.'

'Well, you're very welcome here with me. For as long as you like. We can take care of each other, dear.' She looked over the garden. 'Ernie spent a lot of time out here. Well, here, or in the shed. We didn't talk very much, and I used to think it was like being on my own. It wasn't, though. He was always nearby.'

'You can be quiet, as a couple, and still be good together, I think,' he said.

'Yes. Thank you. That was a helpful thing to say. You've grown up, Raymond.' She looked him up and down. 'Look at you. How long ago was it?'

'Fifteen years.'

'No! Really? I remember when we first moved into this house, and there wasn't a garden as such. It just opened up to the wood, was part of the wood. I was so nervous, every night, thinking something was coming to get me. It's a nasty feeling. Wild animals, leaving their droppings right on the doorstep. So I said – *put up a good strong fence*. And as soon as it was in place I slept better. It doesn't do to think too much about these things, really, Raymond.'

How soothing her voice was, with its meanderings. Ray felt they were reaching a quiet understanding of each other. He risked a question. 'And do you remember what Ernie was like, back then?' he said. 'When you first moved in here? Or when I came to stay? Had he changed a lot since then?'

She cocked her head, and thought.

He wanted her to tell him something personal, like *he fought in the war and never got over it*, or *we lost a child and it changed him*; any of those would have done, to open that line of conversation. Explained something. All he wanted was to reach for an awareness of who Ernie had really been.

'No, no,' she said. 'No, dear. Ernie wasn't here when you stayed in the spare room.'

'He was,' said Ray. 'He was, I remember it.'

'Oh no. But you were young and confused, weren't you?' She turned her bright eyes on him. 'And I wonder if that isn't just the same now, you coming here, and you don't seem to quite know what you're up to, do you? Would it help to tell me what's going on? Why are people looking for you? What's this all about? It's not my business, but I'm happy to listen.'

'I'm…' It was simpler to show her. He put his cup of tea on the arm of the bench and took the Polaroid of Trish from his shirt pocket. Trish, on the beach, on a hot day frozen in his head.

Gwen squinted at it, then held it at arm's length, and nodded. 'Lovely. This is your young lady, is it?'

'That's my wife, Trish.'

'You, married, already? Aren't you a bit young for that, or am I getting old? Well, she looks very glamorous.'

'She's gone.'

Gwen handed back the Polaroid. 'Have you had words?'

He couldn't bottle it up inside any more. 'She said she couldn't, couldn't stand it when I was away, with my job. Months at sea, and then, when I was back – she said she was scared of how I got. But I never hit her, I swear. I never did. And then – she was gone. But not her things. Everything was left as it was. I woke up, I had a bad head. Too much to drink. We'd had an argument, I think. The house was a mess, things broken, but she just wasn't there.'

'You afraid for her, dear?'

'I didn't touch her!'

'No, I mean, she's out there, on her own, then, isn't she? And nobody's heard from her?'

He shook his head. 'She's probably gone to a friend's house. She's making me pay for shouting at her, I know I shouldn't shout but sometimes... I waited for her to come back, but after a few days someone called the police, and then it looked bad. That I hadn't said something before. I didn't know what to do, I had so much stuff in my head. I just...'

She patted his hand. 'Now, now. I know a thing or two about bad tempers, and I know all arguments get smoothed over in the end. She'll come back and all will be forgiven, you'll see.'

'But the police... I'm AWOL–'

'They'll drop it all when they find out what you've been through.'

What did she mean? Was she making a veiled reference to that night, to Mr Latch? 'In that room upstairs...' he started.

'Drink your tea, Raymond, and be still, for a little while. You can stay here with me. Breathe in deep. That's what I do, when I'm thinking too much. That will do you the world of good, too.' She got up, and returned to the house.

*

I never wanted to hurt her. I don't want to hurt her now.

*

There was nothing else to write. Why waste words repeating this stuff? He moved the Polaroid from his pocket to the back of the notebook; it didn't help any more to have it close. He put it and the pen under the pillow, feeling secretive in the dim light thrown from the bedside lamp, then took the towel from his waist and rubbed his hair dry. The bath had been luxurious after so many weeks of cold washes. The bad thoughts had left him completely while he soaked away his cares. He'd never thought to feel so peaceful again.

He examined the pyjamas Gwen had left out for him and decided against them, squeamish about the idea that the last person who had worn them was... well. Ray looked at his naked body. He was softer, less toned. He'd thought living in the woods would be exercise enough, but he realised it had been months since he'd done any proper physical training. No drills, no long runs. The structure of the military, that regimented way of life, was drifting away from him.

Perhaps it was good, to undo what he was.

He knelt down by the side of the bed and put his palms together, his fingers pointing straight up to the ceiling.

'Dear God,' he said.

How strange, to be asking for something. To be in a state of supplication.

'Dear God. Keep them safe.'

Names. He should be specific. God heard so many entreaties.

'Trish. Keep Trish safe, wherever she is. And Mrs Latch. Gwen. Keep her safe from harm. Thank you.'

He got into bed and turned off the light, aware of the boy he had been and still was, of the fear that still found him. Then he remembered the right word to finish speaking to God, and to guarantee that God had listened.

'Amen,' he said.

*

Ray mowed the grass twice a week with the ancient Atco mower, at Gwen's behest. The thin green blades never got the chance to grow.

The sun was hot in the afternoons, and the birds' calls sounded lazier, drowsy, to him. He had run out of cigarettes but found he did not miss them much. Gwen offered him a pipe to smoke and the thought of what pipe she meant to give him disturbed him in ways he could not articulate, much like the pyjamas. He turned her down, and she did not seem to mind.

Still, the occasional feelings of uneasiness provoked by these moments passed, and he enjoyed spending time in the spare room, doing the chores, providing company. It would be easy to fall into the mistake of thinking that was all he was there for, but the need to know the truth about what had happened to him wouldn't quite leave him alone. And so his search for the wardrobe continued.

He had checked every room in the house, including the parlour which never got used and had dust sheets over the furniture. He had even poked into Gwen's bedroom one morning while she was in the outhouse, but the quilted bedcover and the small China knick-knacks on her dressing table had given him no answers. They all looked as if they had stood there for years.

So Ray waited.

He waited for the world to send him a signal. It would not have been a surprise for the doorbell to ring, and for Trish to be on the other side of it, ready to return to their life together, to pick up exactly where they had left off. Such was the soothing power of Gwen's quiet, unstinting support of him, and her reassurances that all would come good, eventually. In time.

*

When the doorbell next rang, it was not Trish.

Ray stood in the kitchen, behind the door, listening to Gwen's voice as she spoke to the interloper; it rose in pitch, a little, but he couldn't detect any annoyance or fear. He stepped into the hall.

'Just for an hour or so,' said a familiar voice, and Gwen replied, 'Oh, of course, of course, he can't be on his own if he's not feeling the best. Come on in, dear.'

'Thanks very much, you're a gem,' said the voice – Trevor, the shopkeeper, that was it, and then the door was opened wide enough to admit the lad, who came in and stood underneath the wall-mounted plates, looking up at them with morose eyes. He was wearing a blue football shirt and white shorts; it was a strange combination with his grey knee-high socks and school shoes.

'Hello,' said Ray. 'You not feeling well?'

The lad shook his head.

'Never mind.'

Gwen closed the door and turned around with her smile for company ready-prepared. 'You poor thing,' she said. 'Do you think you could manage a biscuit? Raymond here will take you to the kitchen to get one, if your tummy is up to it.'

'Yes, please, Miss,' said the lad. The name came back to him in sudden realisation. Jimmy.

She laughed. 'You can call me Mrs Latch,' she said.

'Mrs Latch,' Jimmy repeated, and then Ray led him to the kitchen and took out the biscuit barrel from the cupboard.

'They're only Rich Tea,' he said. 'Usually there are pink wafers, but I've eaten all those, I'm afraid. They're my favourite.'

Jimmy took two, then nibbled at the edge of the first while looking around the kitchen, until Gwen bustled in and said, 'You two gents go off and amuse each other, then,' with an air that would not brook disagreement.

Holt House

The garden seemed the only option. 'Come on,' said Ray, and led the way out into the sunshine.

There was not much to do except sit on the bench, so Ray did that, and Jimmy followed suit.

How slowly time was moving.

'Do you like football, then?' Ray asked him, and then had to wait for a reply while the boy finished a mouthful of biscuit.

'Yeah,' he said.

'Who do you support? That's the Portsmouth strip, isn't it?'

'Portsmouth,' the boy confirmed.

'I'm more of a rugby man, myself.' He racked his brain for other things boys liked. 'You play in the woods, sometimes? Fishing, stuff like that? I used to do that, at your age.' *At your age.* How old he sounded. He wondered if he looked ancient to Jimmy. Foolish, with his stupid questions. He vowed to himself that he wouldn't ask about school.

'Yeah, I like the woods. I go looking for insects and things. Animal tracks. I got a magnifying glass for Christmas, but Dad says not to go far so I haven't found much.'

'That's a shame.' A brainwave came to him. 'Do you like making stuff? You can make something out of wood, in the shed, if you want.'

Jimmy nodded, so they walked down the path and Ray opened the door for him. He didn't shut it, aware that it was a small space; he didn't want the boy to feel uncomfortable.

But Jimmy appeared to be unbothered by having Ray in close proximity. His attention was fixed on the hooks on the wall, and the tools that hung there.

'Is it traps?' he said.

With a closer look, it was obvious. Semi-circular halves bearing curved rows of jagged teeth, closed over a rectangular metal plate – Ray counted four of them. Traps, for catching animals that would be perhaps the size of a terrier. Designed to snap closed on legs, hold the creature in place until the hunter could return.

'They're really old,' he said. 'There are more humane ways of getting rid of pests now.'

'My dad poisoned the rats in the storeroom out the back of the shop. They scratched and scratched. I found a dead one. Is that more... humane?' He seemed unfamiliar with the word.

Ray suspected he should lie, but found himself saying, 'No, no, that would hurt too. They have boxes now, though, the rat goes in, the box closes, then you take it outside and set it free.'

'That's what mum wanted to use. They had a fight about it.'

'Do they fight a lot?' He got the feeling Jimmy wanted to talk about it.

'No. Not now she's gone to live with her new boyfriend.'

'Oh. Right. I'm sorry to hear that.'

'It's okay.'

But it wasn't. Ray could see it, in the lad's face, and it was like being eleven again, and realising his own mother was never coming home. He reached out and gave Jimmy's shoulder a squeeze. 'Women leave,' he said. 'I don't know why, but they leave.'

The boy controlled a sob.

For a distraction, Ray took down one of the traps and showed him the rusty teeth, the pressure plate. 'The animal would put its foot in here,' he said, 'and it would snap shut. Do you want to hold it?'

Jimmy stiffened, ducked his head down. Ray realised he was too close to the lad, bending over him, holding this terrible device close to his young, pale face. He drew back, and the lad vomited, in a rush, throwing up the biscuits down his jumper. Then he pushed past Ray and ran out of the shed, down the path, and back into the house.

Ray put the trap back on the hook.

He would be the last person Jimmy would want to see. He made the decision to let Gwen clean the lad up and entertain him until his dad returned. He would stay in the shed, out of the way.

He tinkered with some offcuts of wood, nailing them together, and waited for time to pass. It seemed like hours before Gwen emerged. He watched her through the window, then left the shed to meet her in the garden, beside the immaculate lawn.

'I'm a bloody idiot,' he said. 'I think I scared him silly.'

'He'll be back,' said Gwen, with such certainty that it was easy to believe her. 'Sit on the bench, dear, and I'll get you a cup of tea.'

Chapter Three

His bladder ached. The pressure was insistent.

If there had been a clock in the room Ray would have checked it, but there were only the usual items, untouched since long before his arrival. Although he practically thought of the room as his, he did not want to move, remove or add anything to it. It suited him just fine as it was, apart from his broken wristwatch which sat on the bedside table; he had caught it against the work bench in the shed while mucking about with bits of wood, and the face had smashed.

He estimated from the light seeping through the gap in the curtains that it was five o'clock-ish, not long past dawn for this time of year. Summer. He was reminded of waking in the tent, where only canvas had separated him from the wild, and birdsong, too insistent to sleep through, had acted as his alarm clock. Each day began early. But now, ensconced in his single bed, he could doze back off, sleep late. Gwen never minded.

No – his bladder wouldn't stand for it. He threw back the blankets, stood up, and stretched.

His jeans were stiff and tight with regular washing. Gwen had pressed a line down the centre of each leg, and the flares were unmoving triangles. He got into them with difficulty – was he putting on weight or was the washing shrinking them? – and threw on yesterday's shirt without bothering to button it, then opened his door.

The landing was silent.

Gwen's door was tightly shut, and he knew her well enough to be sure she would not surface for a while yet. Still, he tiptoed past, and made his way down the stairs to the hall, where the painted eyes of the otters on the plates were fixed upon him. They were so different from the real thing. It had been proud, and strong, gazing at him from the river bank. No, it hadn't been real either. It had been in his imagination. So much had been only in his head. Perhaps the wardrobe had never existed at all.

The grandfather clock ticked on. He glanced up at its face as he passed it. The ornate black hands did keep time: twenty past five. The golden pendulum swayed, visible through the burnished glass case.

Through the kitchen, out into the garden, with the shock of the early morning air on his exposed chest: Ray felt the need to urinate shift from urgent to explosive. He hurried to the outhouse, and locked himself inside, eyeing the cobwebs that had built up overnight behind the cistern. He wasn't fond of spiders, but had yet to see one while he was doing his business. They wisely kept out of his sight.

He finished up, zipped his jeans shut, and pulled the chain. The cistern was still gurgling as he stepped outside and saw him.

Latch.

Latch couldn't be there. But there he stood. The bald head, the braces, the brown slippers.

Ray did nothing.

Latch was not looking at him. He was facing away, his features visible only in profile, while his feet remained pointed in the direction of the house. His attention was on the shed.

'Latch,' said Ray.

There was no response.

It was not fear, there was no fear at all. Shock, yes, at seeing the old man again, and the shock did not want to pass. It felt deep, profound, an expanding sickness that triggered a memory – revulsion. At that night. The wardrobe.

'Latch,' he said, louder. 'What did you do?'

Latch did not move.

'What did you show me?'

A movement. It caught his eye. A man had walked through the fence, and was heading for the shed. For a moment Ray thought it was also Latch; the slippers, the braces, were the same. But this man had hair, although it was fine and white around his head. The face was thinner, the jowls less pronounced.

It was undoubtedly not Latch.

But the clothes were identical.

I'm seeing ghosts, Ray thought.

The second man placed his feet precisely, with a delicacy, as if walking pained him. He had, in one hand, a collection of spent traps, the teeth coated black. In the other hand he held two brown baggy bundles, arms and legs and tails and heads dangling. Drops of red fell, scattering behind him, leaving a trail of blood.

He opened the shed door, went inside, and closed it behind him.

Latch watched the whole thing.

Ray said, 'Why?' He wasn't sure what he meant. He stood very still, tried to think. He had seen Latch's body. The ambulance men, and the distress on Gwen's face; that had all been real, and only weeks ago. He could remember it. The funeral, he couldn't picture. Hadn't he helped to arrange it? Hadn't he attended? He felt certain those things had happened, and yet he couldn't see them in his mind. They were hazy, indistinct, as if they had taken place a long time ago. There had been a service. Yes. A tall, thin Vicar with a beaky nose. Or was that from his mother's funeral? All the past was mixing together.

The second man emerged from the shed, his hands empty. He stretched out his arms to the early morning sunlight, then rubbed his lower back. Ray watched him walk away, back through the fence.

He was gone.

Latch remained where he was, his gaze still fixed upon the shed.

Ray skirted Latch, keeping close to the outhouse, and walked down the path to the shed door. He opened it slowly, just a crack, enough to see inside.

It was empty.

He stepped in, and shut the door behind him.

There, he could breathe. It felt safer.

Was that a clock was ticking? No – the regular sound was dripping. Blood, dripping from the teeth of the traps. It was fresh, the smell strong in the small space. The blood filled Ray's vision; he crouched down, beside the tea chest, closed his eyes, but still there was the sound of dripping, and red everywhere, red behind his eyes and he balled his hands into fists and squeezed, squeezed, until the pain of his fingernails biting into his palm cut through him, and he had to stop.

He opened his eyes.

The traps no longer bore blood upon them. The dripping had stopped.

Ray stood up. He steeled himself, then reached for a trap and took it down from the nail tapped into the wall. It was rusted, rough-textured under his fingers, and the teeth had clamped shut, and lost their sharpness.

Times had changed.

Once, otters had been thought of a pest, and were fair game for whoever wanted to catch them. But Ray couldn't hold the trap and think of it as anything but an instrument of suffering. He put it back on the hook and wiped his palms on his jeans.

A plank from the pile of wood scraps in the corner of the shed clattered to the floor.

Bending to retrieve the plank, Ray saw it: a small, brass keyhole, in one of the remaining planks in the pile. He knew it in an instant. It belonged to the wardrobe.

The wood pile was the remains of the wardrobe.

'There,' he said, then, for some reason, 'Trish.'

He took the piece with the keyhole in his hands. It released no further memories in him. It had been turned into dusty, splintered scrap. Whatever it had been, had meant, was lost to him.

Underneath it – just visible inside the gap left in the pile – was a brown swatch of material. Ray reached in and touched it; it was so soft between his fingers. Fur. He had felt something like it before, retrieved from the river.

He pulled at it, and it moved freely, then caught on something, a nail perhaps. Afraid of tearing it, he widened the gap in the pile, one plank at a time, seeing for the first time how each piece had been placed to create a secret space inside. He found the splintered plank upon which the fur had caught, and removed it. Then he lifted up the fur, and shook it out to reveal a short coat.

It was not an attractive coat, not like the expensive furs models and actresses wore. One shoulder looked bulkier than the other, the buttons were not aligned, and the fur itself was uneven, lumpy. The stitches that held it together were thick, black, and haphazard. So many stitches, for so many otter pelts.

Feel this, Latch had said, and it was like being back there, feeling the man's breath on the back of his neck, *Go on. Put it on your cheek. It's the softest thing. It's otter. I made it.*

Latch pushes forward, thrusts his face into the wardrobe; Ray reacts against the pressure of his hand on his back, but isn't strong enough to escape, and there is a strong, musty smell, like rot, and then the feel of the fur on his face, closing over his nose, filling up his nostrils, blocking the air. He panics, flails, and falls forward – in the dark, the coat surrounds him, engulfs him, and he grabs at it, and sees his mother, his mother being stitched up tight, stitched to death. The coat is bleeding. The coat is alive and squirming in blood.

Whoopsy daisy, Latch says, and then Ray is tugged back, set on his feet, and the wardrobe door is closed, closed shut, and the memory has faded.

Ray held the coat and relived Latch's face, after he was retrieved from the wardrobe. The old man had looked apologetic for what had just happened, and surprised. Red-faced.

It had not been deliberate. Not an attempt to scar him, or make him suffer. Latch had meant him no harm. He had wanted to show off this creation of his, that was all. Like the fort made of wood, and the contents of the shed. Nothing more. And yet it had become something so terrible in his imagination. He had pictured the blood. Perhaps it was not surprising, considering what had been happening to his mother at that time.

But, with the face of Latch clear in his mind, Ray had a clear, certain thought that cut through all the emotions left in the wake of that realisation.

The man who had died on the path a few weeks ago had not been Mr Latch.

Gwen's husband – the man who had shown him the wardrobe – and the man who had died on the path were two different people.

Ray folded the fur coat over his arm, and felt something solid within the material. Feeling inside its folds, pushing down the clear memory of revulsion as its scent filled the shed, he came across an inner pocket with a crude front flap.

He pulled out two books.

Both were small, hard-backed, and musty with age. The first had a title:

Traps and Trapping

Ray flicked through the pages of small print and diagrams, then turned his attention to the second book: small, black, leather, without a title. Inside, the yellowed, crackling pages were filled with neat handwriting. For a moment he thought it was his own; the hand looked like his, and the words were shaped by thoughts to which he felt an immediate connection. There were the carefully spaced letters, and the slope of the script to the left.

He put both books back in the coat pocket, and opened the shed door.

Outside, the men stood, their eyes on him. Five of them, in a line, on the lawn, old and stooped and all dressed the same: shirt, braces, brown leather slippers. Behind them was Holt House, the curtains still shut tight.

They watched him as he walked down the path, the coat pressed against his chest, his heart painful, tight, drumming. He stared back. Latch was there – the one who had held him to the coat in the wardrobe. The one who had died on the path, too. The others, he didn't know.

He turned as he passed them, and walked the rest of the way backwards, feeling his way carefully with his feet. They did not turn in response. They stayed facing the fence, and the woods beyond, as he slipped inside the house and made his way silently back to his room.

*

Ray sat on the single and flipped open the notebook. It bore no name, no dates:

It's a peculiar thing, I'm thinking, for a young man like me to start a journal of his life, but I'm used to being called an odd one. It's not the presumption that one day anybody would want to read it. That's not it in the least.

I was thinking the other day about how, as a boy, I used to make little forts in the woods, with the sticks that had fallen from the trees, with daisy chains for banners and grass blades for soldiers. I never wanted anyone to see what I'd made. I used to spend hours making one, gone from home to the Holtwood on a Sunday, from after church till dinnertime, and then when I returned to the smell of a roast just cooked, or maybe sausages, Mum would ask me what I'd been doing, and I'd say – nothing, Mum.

I always liked to oversee the soldiers in their fort, but I never wanted to be one myself. And, now I think of it, there was never a war in my land of sticks and grass. There was only marching, and lining up for inspection. So that was nothing like what happened when I got called up. Having gone to grammar school made no difference to it at all. I was a private, down in the dirt with the rest of the scared, useless buggers.

Sometimes I still see it, in my mind. The fighting.

Still, I'm not writing a memoir. The war is over and I'm making a fresh start, with my Gwen. Here we are, newly married and in our own house, and a job for me in her father's insurance office. I never thought such a thing would happen to me. I don't feel like I had a hand in it, if I'm honest. She

Holt House

says she always wanted me, from when we were little ones in school together (before I went off to the boys' grammar), so when she saw me at that demob party that was that.

She could have any man, even without her father's money, but she wants me. She cast a spell on me, like they say in the songs. I'm bewitched.

I'm going to get nowhere with this journal if I keep falling into whimsy.

Being married is a funny old business, as is having a house of your own. I keep forgetting I'm the master of Holt House now, and think I shouldn't put my feet on the furniture. Well, I shouldn't really. Gwen doesn't like it. It's all new, bought with the money we were given as a nest egg, and we bought a grand big bed with it, and a dressing set, and all sorts of kitchen things. A Welsh dresser and table and chairs, and a three and two, and even a single bed and a smart wardrobe for the spare room, for when a family starts to come along. That's what Gwen said. I had nothing to bring, nothing that was good enough, but she brought the smart china plates she picked out that she said were perfect for the house, and a grandfather clock that's been in her family forever.

One day, when I start making proper money of my own in the insurance business, I'll give her something good as a wedding present, something just from me to her.

When I speak to her like that, about my private thoughts, she makes a face and says twaddle. I thought women were meant to like all that – getting to know your deep feelings.

Perhaps she'll come round to it. But, for now, I'll make a new fort, just for me. A diary. A fort of words and paper, built from the joy of our marriage. Built to last.

There I go again. Twaddle.

*

Holt House

Holt House – it's a good name for it, here, deep in the Holtwood. I like the way it feels like part of the wood, as if the plants and animals could come right up to the door. It's not been lived in before, having been built by a rich family in London who went bankrupt and lost both sons in the war. Gwen's dad snapped it up for a song. It makes me wonder if somebody's loss is always somebody else's gain, and the world has a balance that won't be appreciated until it all comes to an end.

I mentioned it to Gwen over breakfast yesterday and she said it was beyond her. Then she packed me off to the shed, it being a Saturday. I've got some old tools, now, so the shed is starting to feel like my place. One of the other insurance agents was having a clear out before his retirement and he gave me a big tea chest of his old things, saying a man should have his own bits and pieces. I'm still looking through it, and finding all sorts in there. I set up some shelves and hammered in some nails for hanging things up. It's a man's place now, all right.

I tried to show Gwen but she wouldn't come outside. She says the wood is watching her, and she can hear the wild animals moving about. I've cut it back a fair bit, but she's still not keen. Maybe she's expecting already. I've heard women can come up with funny ideas when they're in the family way.

I should leave her alone, then, until she tells me in her own time, but I can't, I can't, it's out of my control when she puts on that nightdress and lets down her hair. Something comes over me, and I get that feeling I used to get during the war when they were bombing and I just wanted to squeeze and squeeze until it was over. I'd leave big bruises on my own leg, grabbing it and grabbing it, the pain of it would be the only thing that got me through. And now when I'm with Gwen and she's lying there, it builds and builds and before I know it I've got my hands on her neck. She says she doesn't mind, after, and she understands. But still, I shouldn't do it. I know that.

I'll find a way to make it up to her. I'll be gentle, and I won't take advantage of her. I'll do something about the wood, too, to shake her out of her funny thoughts.

*

Holt House

When her father let us have this house, it was on the understanding that he'd have no say in what we did with it. Make it your own – he said. And I'm grateful, of course I am.

Well.

I got home from work and found a pile of new wood, long sawn planks, sat by my shed. A present from father – says Gwen. I ask for what. For a fence. To keep out the woods.

He never once mentioned it to me, at work, or said – what's this about Gwen and the woods? We could have discussed it, man to man.

So now I have to build a fence, and I've got no choice in the matter.

*

I don't mind a fence, if I'm honest. I like to feel that we belong to the Holtwood, because it's always been a safe place to me, but that's neither here nor there. Gwen doesn't sit well with it and that's that. It's only the way it was done that bothers me. If she'd have asked me, I'd have got the wood and built her a fence without prodding.

She's got one of those powder compacts out and is dabbing at her neck as I write. Well, let her. If she doesn't want to be honest with me about her feelings on the matter then I can't help it. I had to ask her out loud, eventually. I said – are we having a child? She blushed, and said – no. I've been tiptoeing around her for months, not even looking sideways at her, and she must have known what I was hoping for. She could have put me out of my misery, but no, she forced me to ask her.

I'll not start on that fence until I'm good and ready.

Down in the shed yesterday I took one of the planks from the pile and cut it to pieces with a saw I got given in that old tea chest. Then I hammered it all together to make a fort, just like I used to make. It was all splintered edges and rough wood, but I'll keep making changes to it and get it how I want it. I wish I had someone to show it off to, if I'm honest, but it will have to be just for me, just like those old grass and stick forts in the Holtwood used to be just for me.

*

Holt House

I'm sorry I argued with her, but she does push me with her silences.

It turns out I'm not much of an insurance salesman. I knew it before her father called me into his office for a chat, of course. Still, he says he'll keep me on and I can do paperwork and make myself useful. He says he's not well, and it'll help to have an extra pair of hands close by.

At the bottom of the tea chest I found four old traps, and a book on trapping. It's given me an idea.

*

The fence is slow work, and she bothers me about it, and it leads to yet more rows, and then I lose my temper, and I'd swear she does it deliberately. But it will all come good once I've got enough pelts. I've been playing around with the traps and reading the book when I'm down the shed.

The book says that otters can be difficult to trap. They're clever. They don't fall for much, but if you place the traps close to each other instead of far apart you stand a better chance. That's because otters have a strong sense of loyalty. So if one gets hurt, and it cries out, others come running to see what's up. That surprises me, I have to say. I thought all creatures ran away from sounds of pain.

It strikes me as cruel, but that's the way of it, otters being pests. Gwen wants all the animals gone apart from the ones on those china plates in the hall. Well, I can't get rid of the wood for her, but I can certainly deal with the otters and give her a nice surprise into the bargain. I'll go out early tomorrow morning and set the traps, just as it says in the book, and see how it goes.

*

Holt House

I couldn't write before this. I couldn't think of words to describe it. The sounds it made, and the way it looked at me. But I want to put it down here, on paper, so it's recorded. Not that I'll ever forget it. I wouldn't want to ever forget it. Some things change you.

I heard it as soon as I stepped out of the house, through the back door. It was faint, but it was there, on the wind that blows from the river. I collected a shovel from the shed and followed it, walking slowly, not wanting to get there. I should have walked faster, but I couldn't bring myself to hurry to it. I didn't want to see what was there, in the trap. The screaming was not like the noise an animal would make. It sounded, to me, like a child in fear, in pain. I was terrified I had caught some young boy while he was out playing, in the woods, and I didn't know what I would do.

So it was a relief to find it, in one way. The screaming stopped when it laid eyes on me, and I saw it watching me with an intelligence to it, even through the state of its front leg. It was a young otter, the size of a cat, and just as clever, I'd say. It looked at me like it knew I'd set that trap, and what I'd done to it.

I was surprised to have caught it, to be honest. It looked too keen to have been lured by the scent of the fish I left out. But then I saw what was in the next trap along — placed nearby as the book suggested — and I understood it. I'd caught an older one first, a fully grown one, and it was dead already, perhaps from the pain. I bet it had called for hours before it died, and this younger one had come to its screams.

I don't know if that's true, of course, but that's how it felt to me, and that's why I hit the young one quick, with the shovel, whacked it on the head twice so the skull was bashed in. So it was done with.

There. That's how it was. Now I won't forget it, how it felt the first time, and it won't bother me so much to go on. I don't seem to be able to hold things in my head so well. Not the bad things. I should remember the sight of bruises on Gwen makes me feel sick, but still I put more there. She never says she minds, that's the thing. She should say it isn't right.

It can't be right.

Skinning them was a delicate business, but the book described it well and I followed the pictures. First I made cuts around all four feet, and down the length of the tail. Then one long cut down each back leg, and I got my fingers up inside and simply pulled the pelt down, like taking off a tight vest in a way, working with my knife in the places where it wouldn't come. It was a good start, but then I reached the head, and had to get the knife further in between the skin and the ears and eyes, and I think I made a right mess of it, but it wouldn't come free, no matter what I did. In the end I simply sliced through those bits, and there was a bit of blood and mess that got on the fur, which the book says should be avoided so as not to spoil the quality of it.

Holt House

Next I have to flesh them. The book tells me how to do that too. I'll work out the cutting and stitching later, and I'll set the traps again tonight.

*

L. G. Vey

It came to me, this morning, over toast and tea, that things have been better between Gwen and me since I started trapping. It takes all the anger out of me.

It's not only that – it's the process of making the skins usable that calms me right down too. I made a wood frame and set it up behind the shed, where Gwen can't see from the house, and I stretched and scraped down the skins there. I started at the neck, using my fingernails, and a whole sheet of fine white fat came off, leaving only the fur behind. It was rhythmic, soothing work, once I got past the smell.

Then I lay the skins in the shed, on the bench, and worked it with my hands, rubbing and rubbing. I used a stone mostly, as the book says to do, but I liked the feel of it on my hands too. I've rubbed my own skin raw in the process, and now I've toughened up, and have a proper working pair of hands. I'm proud of them, and of the way my skins have dried to a loose, supple material I can work with.

Next I'll have to get a needle and thread from Gwen's sewing basket, without her seeing, and have a practice ready for the next bit.

*

Holt House

I have the back and the sleeves made. I took one of Gwen's old bedjackets down to the shed with me, and used that as a guide to getting the shape and size right. I think it's going to be very fine.

I'm reluctant to cut it, is the only thing. Those skins are so precious to me. I can't explain it. But Gwen is more important, and this is my way to show her.

She's still on at me to finish the fence, which is a bit of a sore point between us. It's about half way now, and I'm making a good job of it, too. She says I'm a slow worker, but I like things to be right. I won't bite back at her. I've learned a bit of self control.

It's been all the better for that in the bedroom, too. She asked me the other night, afterwards, if I didn't need to be rough any more. That's how she put it. I said no. She seemed happy with that.

*

It's done.

I've hung up the traps in the shed and I won't be taking them down again. It was hard, to get the final few. I reckon there aren't many otters left in the Holtwood now. Or perhaps they got wise to me, and hid themselves away. I must be a monster to them, and to all the animals in that wood. It felt like they were watching me as I laid my traps, towards the end. I don't think I could bear to set foot inside it again.

But this coat! I made it, and it is a thing of beauty. It's a present fit for her. And I feel older and wiser for having made it. I understand better how to be a proper husband.

I'll give her the coat tonight, after dinner.

*

Holt House

How much time has passed? I don't know. I wrote the last entry in this book in the autumn, and now it's spring again, and the bloody fence is nearly finished and we are still not talking to each other.

There are things we say, of course, like — what's for tea? and — do you want an egg on that? But there are lots of things that don't get a mention. I don't think it's so terrible. Between a husband and wife, memories build up, and some are worth cherishing and some aren't. If we don't talk about the bad ones, perhaps they'll fade.

I'm sitting upstairs writing this while she makes dinner. What was going to be a nursery became a spare room, and then it became my room. It'll never be a nursery now. A couple have to share the same bed to make children.

But I confess I don't want to call it my room. My room and her room. I don't want that.

At the back of the wardrobe, just across from the bed, is the coat I made for her. I gave it to her with such a fanfare: I led her through to the parlour, I poured her a sherry, and I told her I had a present worthy of her. How could it have looked so pretty to my eyes and so ugly to hers? I still don't understand it. She said — take it away Fred, take it away, it smells, and she flapped her hands at it, and demanded it was removed from the house. I had to sneak it back inside, later, and hide it away. I couldn't bear to leave it in my shed.

I made it for you — I told her. A fur coat. Real otter fur. Twenty-three of them.

I can't have it in the house – she said. It's evil. I'm trying to keep all that stuff out. Don't you know me at all?

Evil, that was the word she used.

So it sits in the wardrobe.

I couldn't have been wrong about it entirely, could I? There must be something good in it. I made it. It's a part of me. So there must be.

*

Holt House

The fence is finished.

It's harder to get out the door to go to work. Gwen doesn't seem to mind either way. Since her father's death the business went over to me, but it runs itself if I'm honest. I've had an offer to buy it out from a bigger company, and then we'll be set for life, if we go on as we are. Not going anywhere. Not doing anything.

She's given me my next task. She wants a proper lawn, she says – tidy, respectful. Not growing wild.

I wonder what that means to her. If she realises that you just can't keep all the wildness out. It'll still be there, watching.

She gave me a kiss on the cheek once the fence was finished.

*

I haven't written in so long. I can't even tell how long. I should have put dates on this. When I look back through it, it seems all like it happened yesterday and years ago, all at once.

I can't remember when I last left this house.

I drilled a hole in the fence. Just a little one. I heard voices, and I wanted to see. What was out there, beyond.

It was a father and son, walking past, and the boy was full of excitement. He said — Will we see any, Dad? The father encouraged him — These woods are full of otters, maybe we'll get lucky. Let's try down by the river. Off they went.

I whispered through the hole, after them. You won't see any — I said. I killed them all.

But that was a long time ago. Gwen hasn't spotted the hole. I don't think she sees anything the way I do. I see black, she sees white.

I keep the lawn perfect, and she thinks it's the most beautiful thing in the world. That controlled, restrained cut grass. Nothing grows free in our garden. I sit on the bench and drink my tea, and I do as I am told and I never touch her. I find I don't even want to any more. I think she's the evil one, not me. She's cast a spell on me. I can't leave. I can't think proper thoughts. I'm not a man any more, not a real one. She's taken it from me.

*

Holt House

The boy and his father came round. I've seen them many times since, but I didn't know Gwen had been talking to them. She says they met in the shop, but I can't remember her ever going to the shop. I can't remember much of anything.

The boy's mother was ill, Gwen said, and we had agreed to look after him for the night. He was a scrap of a thing, lost, his mouth all loose and trembling, and he looked nothing like the times I've watched him go past the fence. And I thought I'd cheer him up, and I took him down to the shed and showed him the fort I'd made.

Then I remembered he'd been looking for otters, and it seemed sad to me that he'd never touch one. The fur is so soft. So I took him upstairs and opened the wardrobe. It was such a lark to show it off, and to think that finally somebody would appreciate it. Well, I should say, I thought it would be and perhaps that meant I wasn't paying enough attention to what the boy thought of it all.

He fell forward, and I caught him by the back of his jumper, and set him back on his feet. The look he gave me. He was afraid of me. I felt sick to my stomach, about it, after, when I'd had time to think.

I'm an idiot.

If I overbalanced him, if I was too keen to get him to touch that coat, then I'm sorry for it, more sorry than I can say. It makes me wonder: am I so unlovable, so ugly inside? If I am it's because of her. Because she makes me that way. She won't love me.

No, I didn't mean to push the boy, I'm certain of it. It was an accident, and he'll realise that when he thinks about it. I do feel for him, though, for he lost his mother that night too. His father told him when he came to pick him up, and I thought back to those first otters, in the traps. Suffering together.

The endless days in this house. I have to leave.

I have to leave.

I have to leave.

*

She is something not human. She sucks all time and hope and love out of me.

I told her I was going, and she patted my hand, and said – how would you do without me, dear? She looks at me and I feel weak. Everything I have made for her, tried to be for her, she destroys with her words. I go to the shed and keep the lawn every day, and I get nothing for it.

But when I look through the hole in the fence I don't recognise the wood any more. I whisper to it – help me. Help me. But it's not my friend. It's been my enemy. I made an enemy of it, for her.

And, in return, she's made me so old. My hair, my face, my body – how can an elderly man survive out there, in that strange world?

Where did the time go?

*

L. G. Vey

I heard her get up in the night, and go downstairs. I'd been awake for hours, thinking things through, making my plans to leave. Often I think about how different our married life would have been if she had simply and clearly told me no the first time I squeezed her throat. Because I think that is when she first started to hate me, and cast her spell. If she had said no, I would have stopped. It would have been that simple.

I don't know what made me get up and go down to her. Perhaps I thought we could talk to each other, in the dark, properly. Like people.

When I got down to the kitchen, walking past the beady eyes of all those painted otters on her precious plates, she was sitting at the table with a glass of water in front of her. She'd turned on the parlour light but the kitchen was still in darkness. I couldn't see her face, her expression.

I asked what she was up to.

It's funny, how I whispered that question. Something about the tick of the clock, the blackness of the night outside the window, made me keep my voice low. And when she replied, her voice was very soft, too.

I was thirsty – she said. I couldn't sleep. I suppose I'm worrying about things.

Like what? – I asked her. I pulled out the chair opposite, and sat down. The house was cold, what with winter approaching. I wished I'd put on my dressing gown.

Oh Fred.

That was all she said.

78

Holt House

I couldn't bear it. I still can't. It was pity I heard, in her voice. She pitied me. I got up and went back to bed.

So I've made plans to leave. I've put together some things, and I'll go. I'm going. Before I'm no longer a man at all.

*

The remaining pages were blank.

Ray put the book down on top of the fur coat. For all of Fred's words, it was obvious that the man had never left. He was still there.

There was Ernie, too.

And the others.

He got up and crossed to the window, pulling the curtain aside just enough to see down into the garden. It was empty. The blades of grass that made up the lawn were upright and keen, and the weeds did not dare intrude amongst them.

A flash of blue caught Ray's eye, moving fast, beyond the line of the fence. An animal? No – a man, walking in a crouch, almost hidden by the dense summer foliage of the cherry trees except for his blue football shirt.

The man disappeared from view.

He had been at the fence line. He had been using the hole to look at the house. To look at him and Gwen.

Ray dropped the curtain, stumbled back to the bed. His breath wouldn't come easily.

'Breakfast!'

Gwen's voice broke through his thoughts, dragged him back to the morning. But it made no sense that it was already breakfast time – he hadn't even heard her get up, and just a moment earlier it had been dawn. Time was a muddle. Time was under her control.

His hands were trembling. He clasped them together in his lap, and saw deep wrinkles in the skin, and a bluish tinge to the blunt nails. They were the hands of an old man.

'Breakfast, dear!' There was an unmistakable edge of irritation to her voice.

He pushed the coat and the journal under the bed. He would find a better hiding place for them later.

*

'Oh good,' she said, as he took his seat opposite her. The toast was in the rack and the teapot on the table, waiting for him. She poured as he took up the butter knife. 'Did you sleep well?'

'Not so bad,' he said.

'I thought I heard you moving about early.'

'Just a visit to the loo.'

'Will you mow the lawn for me today, dear?'

'I did it yesterday, didn't I?' he said, but the memory wasn't clear. He couldn't keep his voice even, but she gave no sign of hearing anything unusual.

'It gets straggly so quickly. I don't like it when its straggly. It grows so fast, doesn't it?' She turned in her chair to look back towards the sink, and out of the window. Although he couldn't see her expression he had no doubt she was frowning.

'It's the summer,' he said. 'Isn't it?'

'Is it?' She swivelled back to face him, and poured herself more tea.

'What year is it?'

'Goodness, what a question. Do you know, I want to say 1946. That's the first one that comes into my head. But that was the year we moved in here, of course, so. That must be why.'

'You and Fred moved in here.'

'That's right.'

'Not Ernie.'

'No, of course not Ernie, dear.'

'And Fred died. What year was that?'

'Are you finished with that, Raymond?' She stood up, and took his plate to the sink. She was an expert in stonewalling him; what had once seemed like the confusion of a little old lady now struck him as a deliberate attempt to avoid questions she didn't care to answer.

'How did Fred die?' he said.

'Isn't it a bit early in the morning for all this? Let's have a glass of sherry tonight and then we can have a good old natter about it all, can't we?'

'Just tell me how he died.'

'A heart attack, I think they said. The men who came to take him away.'

Ray got up, and joined her at the sink. The shed was still in the shade, but the lawn was in full sunlight. It was going to be a glorious day. Too hot for sitting on the bench, mowing the lawn, being brought endless cups of tea... He felt a vast pit of frustration open inside him for this life, this sham of life at Holt House. The Holtwood would be cool, shaded. The river would be running, winding its way through the Meon Valley, all the way to the sea, the blue, open sea.

'A heart attack,' he repeated. 'By the outhouse.'

She was very small beside him as she looked up and said, 'No, no. In bed. In your room, dear. Well, that was his room, back then. We had separate rooms, you see.'

'He died – in that bed?'

She nodded, and turned the tap to run water into the sink.

'So... who was the man who died by the outhouse? On the path that morning?'

There was a flash of recognition in her eyes – a glimpse of the sharp mind underneath her act, he thought. 'That was Ernie. Number four. No, number five, excuse me, I'm losing count. It's the old age, isn't it?'

'Ernie. Number five.'

The five men in the garden. The ghosts. So alike.

'First there was Fred,' she said. 'Then George. Philip, then Joseph. I don't care for shortened names. I made an exception for Ernie, only because he was so adamant that he hated being called Ernest. He said his ex-wife used to call him that when he'd done something wrong, deliberately, knowing how it wound him up. And now you. Raymond.'

'So I'm – number six?'

'You are, dear.'

'How do you know? I just – I just turned up on your doorstep. You barely knew me, but you let me in, you let me in, but I'm not, I'm not–'

'You were watching,' she said. 'Weren't you?' Her hands were busy in the sink, washing the plate, the same plate, over and over. 'The hole in the fence. You saw Ernie die. And then it was your time to come. The young one comes because the old one calls through the fence. They think I don't see them, crowding there, putting their eyes and mouths to that hole. But I do. I see all the things they get up to.'

'I'm not–' he said again. Not what? He could leave, walk out. He wasn't a wild animal, caught in a trap, drawn to this place by the cries of another like him. He didn't have to be here.

'You want to go,' Gwen said. 'I wish you would. Go away. Go on. Leave me alone, all of you. But you can't, can you? I know what you are. I know your nature. All I wanted to do was keep it out, keep it at bay, but no, you have to bring it in. You have to bring it in with you.'

'Stop it,' he said. 'Stop it.' But she worked on at the plate, washing, the water sloshing in the sink. He lifted his hand and put it on her throat, just above her collarbone. Her skin was cold, loose. It repulsed him, but he did not take his own hand away – so wrinkled, spotted brown, the nails thick and ridged, Jesus, he was aging before his own eyes – nor did he apply pressure. It was enough to touch her, to know he could touch her. He could make her be quiet. It was within his power.

She did not move away. She did not look at him. She put the plate on the drainer, softly.

'That's right,' she said.

He dropped his hand and stepped back.

'I'm going,' he said.

'That's good. See if you can do without me.'

He walked, fast, to the hall, his thoughts focused on his tent in the Holtwood. He could return to it, crawl inside it, be safe and small and alone, like a dormouse. He didn't stop to collect his backpack; he simply opened the front door and found a grey, unremarkable day happening outside. It was cool and threatening rain, and was nothing like the sunshine he had seen pouring through to the back garden.

He walked down the path and out of the gate. Then around the house, thinking it looked small, dull, in profile. Moss and lichen had spread over the brickwork on this side, where the sun did not shine. His footsteps squelched on the dirt path, lined with abundant weeds which must have sprung up quickly; he could not remember seeing them when first approaching the house.

The Holtwood came into view, as beautiful and tangled as ever, thick with cherry trees, but the leaves were brown and limp on the branches, and many had fallen to coat the ground. It was cold. There was a nip in the air, to the drops of rain, that he associated with late autumn. And yet in the house it had been summer, high summer, warm and bright.

Don't turn back, he told himself.

He pressed on, into the woods. His breaths came fast, his lungs hurting from the effort of walking. Onwards. Leaving the fence behind, refusing to look back at the spot where he had once crouched, imagining himself inside. He retraced his steps and found the small clearing where he had left his tent, packed up and stowed under a small leafy bush.

Except the bush wasn't so small any more. He recognised the dark green foliage, but it had spread into the clearing, growing over the available ground, so he found a stick nearby and hacked, making a path through it. Tightness in his chest, dizziness, forced him to stop. He bent double, his hands on his knees, and tried to control his growing panic. His stomach pressed against the top of his jeans; he undid the top button and the zip, and felt the curve of the flesh there, loose, saggy.

Deep, slow breaths.

Eventually his vision cleared and his lungs stopped hurting.

Ray inched forward through the bush to reach the spot where he had left his tent. There it was, nearly buried under old, wet leaf and mould growth, the canvas packed tight, the small bag that held the pegs still attached.

Holt House

He pulled it from the bush and clutched it to him, fighting back tears of relief. *What a bloody idiot*, he thought. *To be so pleased to see a tent.*

A scream cut through the air.

No – a siren. Another siren, just like that morning he had seen Ernie dead on the path. Were they still searching for him? Caught in the grip of memory, he set off for the river once more.

*

The siren ended as quickly as it had begun, leaving the wood silent and watchful around him.

The water flowed, winding its way down through the valley to join the sea. Ray wanted his father. He wouldn't have been surprised if his father had simply walked out from the trees to stand beside him, and tell him that they would surely see an otter today. He should be watchful, and keep his distance. He felt so young, as if he had learned nothing from that moment to this.

He reached up to his hair, smoothed it back, and felt how brittle and thin it had become. He had not shaved in months, had he? But when he ran his hand over his cheeks there was only a downy fluff rather than a beard.

There were no otters to be seen, of course.

A twig snapped, close by; Ray jerked his head around to the sound, on his side of the river, and saw a flash of bright blue. His first thought was of the kingfisher, but no – this was bigger, moving up and down in jerky motions. It took him a moment to realise he was looking at a blue shirt. A man was walking away from him, through the wood.

A blue shirt. Just like the one the man he had seen from the window had been wearing. Like the one Jimmy had worn.

Ray followed, trying to keep pace, puffing with the effort, keeping that glimpse of blue at a decent distance. The temptation was to call out a name: Jimmy. But this was a man, not a boy. Jimmy had been a boy a few days ago. It was too much; Ray pushed the name out of his mind, refused to speak it. They were drawing closer to the edges of the wood. The trees came to an abrupt end and Ray hung back as the man stepped out into the grey light, and stood beside a road that had simply not been there before.

Ray edged as close as he dared, then hid behind a tree, clinging to the rough reality of the bark, and watched the man pull out a small box from the pocket of his jeans and tap on it.

A car arrived at a speed that was breathtaking. It came to a halt easily beside the man. But it wasn't exactly a car; more like a cross between a car and a motorbike: two wheels, with a domed roof and no doors, only big enough for one person. The vehicle itself made no noise – there was no low idle to the motor. Nobody was driving it.

Ray shook his head in disbelief.

The man climbed in and spoke, apparently to the vehicle. 'Intruder spotted at the Holtwood reserve. Possible poacher. Elderly,' he said. 'There's been a spate of it recently, since the new rationing came in.' There was a pause. 'It could be Latch, although they've been told they're only allowed to stay on the condition they don't enter the woods. I know the family, a little. I grew up around here. I'll check in on it.'

The vehicle sped up as quickly as it had arrived, taking the man away.

Ray moved to the very edge of the woods and looked out at the road, fighting down his fear of it, of the speed at which the vehicle had travelled. In the distance was the village, so silent. On the other side of the road was a white sign with red lettering upon it:

Holtwood and immediate surroundings
EVACUATED AREA
via 1992 Wildlife Pollution Protection Act
Unique intact environmental region
No entry permitted
Private security forces operate in this area

He turned and plunged back into the woods, moving as fast as he could. The tent was too heavy to carry so he dropped it, left it behind without hesitation, and only stopped running when the river came back into view and his lungs and legs screamed to rest.

The water flowed on: he had the idea to follow it down to Portsmouth, out to the sea. Would the world make any more sense to him there? A sudden movement made him spring back from the bank; he stared into the undergrowth, but could see nothing.

It wouldn't hang around for you to point him out. Otters are fast. So fast. All the other animals are afraid of them, did you know that? They're carnivores, with teeth that can go through bone.

The fallen leaves trembled with the breeze. The branches swayed overhead.

Move, he told himself.

He started forwards, taking small steps, scanning the ground. Were they behind him? He refused to give into the instinct to turn around. The wildness was everywhere, surrounding him. The Holtwood was alive, full of animals, and he did not belong. Nobody did, any more.

Keep going.

There, in the distance, was the strong straight line of the Latches' fence – the same as it always was. Ray picked up his pace, reached it, put his hands upon it. He pushed a finger through the hole, then put his eye to it. It was light, and still, and perfect inside. The lawn was green and freshly cut, and the bench was waiting for his return.

He edged around the fence, making his way towards the front of the house, unable to turn and face the woods.

The gate, the path, the front door.

He turned the handle and, thank God, it opened, and there he was, back in Holt House, and as soon as he closed the door his fear, that emasculating fear, began to ebb away. All he could hear was the slow ticking of the grandfather clock in the darkness of the hall. He took deep breaths, in time, until he was calmer.

In the kitchen, glorious sunshine poured through the back window.

Gwen was nowhere to be seen. Perhaps she was upstairs. How much time had passed since he left? He moved to the back door and out through the porch, then along the path to the shed. It was the only place left where he belonged.

*

Inside the shed, he crouched, his back against the old tea chest, the traps hanging above him.

He hadn't realised how much he had come to rely on its jars and tools, dusty corners and scrap wood, to keep him safe. He picked two pieces of wood from the pile, then took down a hammer and a nail, and put his mind entirely to the task of making something. It didn't matter what. Maybe it was a boat. It looked like a boat, to him.

After a time – he had no idea how much time – there was a knock on the door. He jumped, held up the hammer in front of him, but she didn't come in.

'Sorry dear, I know you're busy in there, but I just wanted to say – your old clothes, I noticed at breakfast – they're getting a bit small for you, aren't they? I've sorted out some bits and pieces you can wear instead. I'll leave them just outside the door here. And we'll have that sherry later, won't we?'

So no time had passed at all.

He watched from the window as she left. Once he was certain she was back in the house, Ray opened the door, just enough to see what she had placed there, at the end of the path.

A white shirt. Braces. Corduroy trousers.

Brown leather slippers: old, creased, lived in. But good for a few years yet, no doubt Gwen would say. Good for a few years yet.

Chapter Four

At the end of the day, after a shepherd's pie eaten in silence, Ray admitted defeat. The jeans were too uncomfortable to wear any longer. He went upstairs and changed into the clothes Gwen had given him.

Without a mirror, it was difficult to tell whether he had been transformed entirely into one of her men, but he was glad of having no means to check. His hands, his stomach, the bits of himself he could see, were changed: he had to admit that. But maybe his face remained his own. As long as he believed that, he thought maybe he had a chance to escape back to his own time.

There had to be a way to break this spell.

He pulled out the coat of otter fur, and Fred's abandoned journal and the book on trapping, from under the bed. Then he retrieved his own notebook from under the pillow and wrote a final message.

I'm caught between the woods and the witch.

If I don't make it out of here, back to where I belong, and you find this book then I'm so sorry, Jimmy. I didn't mean to call you here. We're all caught up in traps we don't understand.

Where to hide it? Eventually he shifted the single bed and found a loose edge to the carpet; he placed the books flat against the floorboards, and then replaced the carpet and returned the bed to its original position so that nothing looked out of place.

The otter coat, he put over his arm, smoothing the thick pelts, feeling the rough, ugly edges of the stitching. Then he started down the stairs to Gwen.

*

The parlour had been stripped of dust sheets and opened up for the special occasion.

She had already poured two schooners of cream sherry, and placed them on the low glass-topped table in front of the unlit fireplace, logs arranged in an orderly stack. The lamp with the damask pink shade, standing in the corner, had been switched on to give a soft, subdued light. In it Gwen looked younger: her cheeks were rouged, her dress seemed a little more shapely. She had made an effort for him.

This was the first time Ray had seen the rose-pattern of vibrant red blooms on the cream three and two, unfaded, with scrolled oak arms. He sat next to her on the smaller sofa, and placed the otter coat across his lap.

When she saw it, her eyes rolled and her lips pulled back from her teeth in a grimace; then she collected herself, pulled her expression straight, and said, 'Raymond, where did you find that old thing?'

'In the shed. Under the remains of the wardrobe. You know, the wardrobe that used to stand in my room.'

She nodded. 'I always did wonder what he did with it. I asked him to destroy it, you know.'

'I know. I read his diary. That was in the pile under the wardrobe, too.'

She cocked her head. 'The diary, yes! So that's where he put it. I remember him writing in it when we were first married. After he came back – from trying to leave me, you know – he dragged that wardrobe down to the shed and broke it into pieces, and hid his guilty secrets underneath it. He was a funny one, in lots of ways. I don't think I ever understood him. I don't understand any of you.'

'Men, do you mean?' asked Ray.

'I wonder if you wouldn't mind putting the coat down, perhaps by the door there, so I can get rid of it later. I do so hate having it in the house.'

He obliged. It had done the trick. She had been caught off guard by the coat, and had revealed something of her real self. He felt he had a chance to break her spell, having a better idea of who she really was. So she didn't understand men – perhaps that could be used to his advantage. He put the coat by the parlour door and returned to his seat.

The sherry spread a warmth through him; the night was cooler than he had been expecting. Autumn was on its way, he would have said, once, back when he understood how time worked.

'How do you do it?' he asked.

'Do what, dear?'

'Trap us. Keep us. Turn us old.'

'Oh Raymond. You never do learn, do you? None of you. It's not me.'

'It's some kind of spell. It's…' The thought dawned on him: what if she was telling the truth? He no longer knew what to believe – could Fred have been mistaken, in his journal? 'So tell me what you think keeps us here. Is it the house?'

She shook her head. 'It's just a house on the edge of a wood I never cared for, and what a fuss you've all made of that over the years. You think I want the wood gone, all the creatures in it dead. Not at all. I love nature. I even love animals, in their rightful place. But what the wood brought out in you all, yes, I wanted that gone, of course. That wildness in you.'

'You mean the men who had lived here with you,' he said, feeling heat in his cheeks from the alcohol. 'We're not all the same man. I'll be the last of it. I'm bringing an end to it. Tonight.'

'Raymond, that's a lovely thought. But I already know you're not the last, and you do too, don't you? Little Jimmy, coming to visit, and there are others after him, I've already seen them.'

Holt House

'Seen them?'

'They don't leave, do they? Ones from the past, ones from the future. It's all the same thing in this house. The dates make no difference. You saw that, outside. What did you see? A funny world, isn't it, the future? It looks like a desperate place, with the people all thrown out to make way for that wood, and signs saying they can't be hunted, can't be eaten. That it's better if people go naked and starve. Well, that's not your future, anyway, is it? You'll be just like one of them, soon enough, just standing around on my lawn.' Gwen sipped her sherry, sitting up straight, prim. How she loved giving him these answers, piecemeal, telling him whatever she chose to. It wasn't right for a woman to have that kind of power over a man. 'Perhaps it's the price you have to pay, for what you are.'

'What are we?'

'Killers,' she said. 'You're a killer, Raymond. You killed your wife.'

'I didn't,' he told her. 'She left me.'

She lifted her schooner of sherry, now half-emptied from her sipping; it slopped in the glass and he realised she was already a little tipsy. 'Fred was a killer too, but at least he had the war as an excuse. The rest of you took it out on your wives, those poor ladies. I suppose the only good thing is that they got to escape you. I'm stuck with you.'

'I never killed her,' he said, his voice rising – he couldn't help it, didn't know how to stop himself from shouting.

'You're wild animals. Ernie killed his own children too, when he found his wife had taken up with another man. Imagine that. He blocked it out, of course, pretended it hadn't happened, and I can't blame him, or you, for that. It must be so much easier to be able to say *she left me*, or *I don't remember*. But you'll remember, before the end. They always do.'

But Trish had left him. Trish had left him, he had woken and found her gone, he was sure of it, and the wood – the Holtwood had seemed like the only place where he could hide. Until it turned against him. 'The Holtwood,' he whispered. 'That's what causes this. That's what traps me here.'

'No, no, no,' Gwen snapped. 'You're always so ready to blame someone else, anything else. But it's you. You're making this happen.'

'I didn't – I never…' He smashed down his glass on the table, and stood up.

'You want to leave.'

'Yes, but–'

'You want to leave, but you're afraid. Afraid of what you are outside. An old man, alone, and you can't be alone, can you? That's why you killed her. Because she wanted to leave you.'

The arguments. His insistence that she should not leave the house. *You belong here. You can't leave.* But women leave; they find one way or another, like his mother. Like

Holt House

Trish, with her bags packed and pushed under the bed, and he had found them. The things we all hide, under the bed, down in the shed. *I can't live like this any more*, she says and that, that is what pushes him over the edge, she knows it, she knows what she's doing when she needles him like this, and his hands find her throat.

Yes that's right, says a voice from far away, and he squeezes, and squeezes.

This is how it is. This is who he is. He surrenders to his strength, the screams, to the bite of the trap.

He kills her. He kills her all over again.

*

The grandfather clock had stopped ticking.

Ray came to, looked around himself.

He was still in the parlour. His back was against the wall by the door, and the otter coat was next to him. The rose-hued light from the lamp shone down.

Gwen's hand was poking out over the arm of the sofa. Her wrist faced the ceiling, and her fingers were curled into a tight bud of a fist.

He stood up, and looked at her face. The bloodshot eyes, the dark red mouth, the black tongue protruding. The thick mottled marks where he had put his hands. She looked, in this pose, much as Trish had looked.

Women had so much in common.

He heard birdsong outside and wandered into the kitchen to stand by the sink, looking out over the dawn. The others were there, together, on the perfect green expanse of the lawn, facing the fence. They all looked so similar in the same clothes – the clothes he was wearing. Some of them were only suggestions of men, flickering, as if waiting to be brought into being. The possibilities of men to come.

There were more than five of them. They filled the lawn, standing shoulder to shoulder. There were too many to count.

He went outside, and they turned their empty expressions to him and moved aside to let him pass. The dew of the lawn soaked into his brown slippers, then through the knees of his trousers as he reached the fence, and knelt, and put his eye to the hole. Beyond, the wood was white, alive with movement, branches dancing in snowfall, time moving differently. Who knew what year it was, out there? All he could see was that it was winter. He put his finger through, and felt the icy cold penetrate it. He pulled it back to the sunshine.

'Help me,' he whispered through the hole, hating himself, but he couldn't stop it. Gwen was right about him. He had no control over his actions. He was an animal. 'Please God. Please. Don't leave me here, alone. Make her stay. Make her stay.'

'Raymond!'

He swivelled at the sound of her voice, lost his balance, sat back on the grass.

'Breakfast, dear,' she said, from the porch, looking the same as ever, unchanged in every way. She returned to the house.

Gratitude flooded over him; she had not left him. She was not like the other women. She had stayed. How had she managed that? It had been a prayer. A prayer answered. His heart hurt with the thought of it.

He walked through the ghosts of the other animals and returned to the house.

Holt House

Join the Society

The Eden Book Society is an ongoing book subscription brought to you by Dead Ink Books. Each book is written by a different author under a pseudonym and each year we select a different year from the society's history to reproduce. There's even a secret newsletter for subscribers only from our resident archivist digging through the Eden family records.

The 1972 books are written by: Andrew Michael Hurley; Alison Moore; Aliya Whiteley; Jenn Ashworth and Richard V. Hirst; Gary Budden; and Sam Mills.

If you would like to subscribe to The Eden Book Society please visit our website.

www.EdenBookSociety.com

The 1972 Subscribers

In 1972 the subscribers to the Eden Book Society were...

Adam Lowe
Adam Rains
Adam Sparshott
Adrienne Ou
Agnes Bookbinder
Aki Schilz
Alan Gregory
Alexandra Dimou
Alice Leuenberger
Alison Moore
Aliya Whiteley
Amanda Faye
Amanda Nixon
Andrew Pattenden
Andy Banks
Andy Haigh
Anna Vaught
Anne Cooper
Anthony Craig Senatore
Ashley Stokes
Audrey Meade
Austin Bowers

Barney Carroll
Becky Lea
Ben Gwalchmai
Ben Nichols
Ben Webster
Benjamin Achrén
Benjamin Myers
Blair Rose
blutac318
Brian Lavelle
C Geoffrey Taylor
C. D. Rose
Catherine Fearns
Catherine Spooner
Cato Vandrare
Chris Adolph and Erika Steiskal
Chris Kerr
Chris Naylor-Ballesteros
Chris Salt
Christopher Ian Smith
Clare Law

Colette

Conor Griffin

Damian Fuller

Dan Coxon

Daniel Ross

Dave Roberts

David Harris

David Hartley

David Hebblethwaite

Debbie Phillips

Dennis Troyer

Derek Devereaux Smith

Edward S Lavery

Elizabeth Nicole Dillon

Christjansen

Elizabeth Smith

Eloise Millar

Emily Oram

Eric Damon Walters

Erik Bergstrom

Erin C

Ex Somnia Press

Fat Roland

Françoise Harvey

Gareth E. Rees

Gemma Sharpe

Gia Mancini McCormick

Gina R. Collia

Green Hand Bookshop,
Portland, ME

Gregory Martin

Hannah allan

Harry Gallon

Hayley Hart

Heather Askwith

Helen de Búrca

Ian McMillan

Imogen Robertson

Inés G. Labarta

Jack Hook

James Smythe

Jamie Delano

Jamie Lin

Jayne White

Jean Rath

Jen Hinton

Jen Lammey

Jenna H.

Jennifer Bernstein

Jennifer Rainbow

Jim Ryan

Jo Bellamy

John P. Fedele

Jon and Rebecca Cook

Jon Peachey
Joseph Camilleri
Joshua Bartolome
Joshua Cooper
Justine Taylor
Karen Featherstone
Kate Armstrong
Kate Leech
Kathryn Williams
Kelly Hoolihan
Ken Newlands
Kiran Milwood Hargrave
Kirsty Mackay
Laura Carberry
Laura Elliott
Lee Rourke
Livia Llewellyn
Louise Thompson
Lucie McKnight Hardy
Madeleine Anne Pearce
Mairi McKay
Majda Gama
Margot Atwell
Maria Kaffa
Mark Gerrits
Mark John Williamson
Mark Richards

Mark Scholes
Martin van der Grinten
Matt Brandenburg
Matt Neil Hill
Matt Thomas
Matthew Adamson
Matthew Craig
Michael Cieslak
Michael Paley
Mitch Harding
Nancy Johnson
Naomi Booth
Naomi Frisby
Nathan Ballingrud
Nici West
Nick Garrard
Nick Wilson
Nicola Kumar
Nikki Brice
Nina Allan
Owen Clements
Paul Gorman
Paul Hancock
Paul Tremblay
Peter Farr
Peter Haynes
Philip Young

Ray Reigadas
Rhiannon Angharad Grist
Rhodri Viney
Richard Grainger
Richard Kemble
Richard Sheehan
Ricki Schwimmer
Rob Dex
Robb Rauen
Robert P. Goldman
Robin Hargreaves
Robyn Groth
Rodney O'Connor
Rudi Dornemann
Ruth Nassar
S. Kelly
Sanjay Cheriyan Mathew
Sarah R.
Sardonicus
Scarlett Letter
Scarlett Parker
Simon Petherick
Sophie Wright
Spence Fothergill
Stephanie Wasek
Steve Birt
Steven Jasiczek

STORGY Magazine
Taé Tran
Tania
Terra & Bill Jackson
The Contiguous Pashbo
The Paperchain Podcast
Thom Cuell
Thomas Houlton
Tim & Meg
Tim Major
Timothy J. Jarvis
Tom Clarke
Tom Jordan
Tom Ward
Tony Messenger
Tracey Connolly
Tracey Thompson
V Shadow
V. Ganjanakij
Verity Holloway
Vince Haig
Wheeler Pryor
Yvonne Singh
Zoe Mitchell

Coming Soon...

Starve Acre
Jonathan Buckley

Richard and Juliette Willoughby live in an old farmhouse somewhere in North Yorkshire. The place has been called Starve Acre since anyone can remember and there is a local story about there being 'something' buried in the field. A 'something' which prevents anything from growing there. Quite what it is varies from one person to the next – a witch, or some tool once used by a witch, or the rope used to hang a witch – but there is general agreement in the area that it is a place to be avoided. In fact, the locals blame Starve Acre for Juliette's illness, a degenerative mental condition that has transformed her into a vacant, ghost-like shell of her former self..

A Dedicated Friend
Shirley Longford

Organ donation is in its infancy and Daisy Howard, who is giving a kidney to her aunt, is in the hands of a pioneering surgeon. After the operation, Daisy is desperate to get back to her family, yet the days go by and she remains in the hospital; meanwhile, an old friend keeps visiting with news of home, and Daisy becomes increasingly uneasy.

Plunge Hill: A Case Study
J.M. McVulpin

'Dear Maurice, I'm writing to you by candlelight again. Another power cut. I had to carry the papers back and forth in the dark, tiny flames flickering in the stairwells... They've got the petrol generators running in Ward 7 and the noise they make is like a swarm of bees has got into the place...'

In 1972, during the chaotic days of miners' strikes and the three-day week, Bridget 'Brix' Shipley moves to Plunge Hill to start her new job as a medical secretary at the local hospital. As she writes to Maurice, her younger brother, sick at home, it becomes clear that not all is well at Plunge Hill. There are frequent power cuts and she has to work by candlelight. While she'd hoped this might inspire some blitz spirit and solidarity between her, the other secretaries and the medical staff, she's increasingly isolated and seemingly ignored by her co-workers.

Judderman
D.A. Northwood

London, early-1970s. In a city plagued by football violence, Republican bombings, blackouts and virulent racism, a new urban myth is taking hold. Among the broken down estates, crumbling squats and failed projects of a dying metropolis, whispered sightings of a malevolent figure nicknamed the Judderman are spreading. A manifestation of the sick psyche of a city, or something else?

The Castle
Chuck Valentine

Jon's dad was something of a pioneer in 1972, after writing a new kind of book – a book where readers could make their own choices and choose their own way through the story. Unfortunately, the idea was ahead of its time and his father died without ever finding the success he deserved.

It's the summer and, between signing on to the unemployment allowance, Jon's moved back to his hometown to help his mum cope with her grief. Contending with his own grief, he loses himself in his father's unpublished manuscripts. Fiction and reality blend perhaps a little too closely, and when he discovers a hidden appendix he finds that his father's imagination was more terrifying and more powerful than he could have imagined.